JUDGING THE JUDGE

"I have reason to believe, Kelso, that Judge Boller shot his wife to death last night."

Silence, while Kelso considered this. He waited expectantly, unable to believe what Leill had said but ready to hear his reasons for it.

"This is an extremely sensitive situation, Kelso. Judge Boller's not merely a criminal court judge. He's an important man politically. There's even been talk of his running for office, possibly senator or representative. He has connections." Leill cleared his throat loudly. "Do you follow me so far, Kelso?"

"Yes, sir." Kelso kept his voice neutral while one thought raced through his mind: *Cover-up.*

Other Avon Books by
Malcolm McClintick

DEATH OF AN OLD FLAME
MARY'S GRAVE

THE KEY

MALCOLM McCLINTICK

AVON BOOKS NEW YORK

All of the characters in this book are fictitious, and any resemblance to actual persons, living or dead, is purely coincidental.

AVON BOOKS
A division of
The Hearst Corporation
105 Madison Avenue
New York, New York 10016

"A Crime Club Book"

Published by arrangement with Doubleday, a division of Bantam Doubleday Dell Publishing Group, Inc.
Library of Congress Catalog Card Number: 87-10114
ISBN: 0-380-70819-1

First Avon Books Printing: May 1990

Printed in the U.S.A.

RA 10 9 8 7 6 5 4 3 2 1

To Beth Bandy, and to the memory of her husband and my friend, Frank

One

The judge's wife stood in the hall doorway with her hands at her hips, staring at her husband, searching for words. She was thinking that after seventeen years of marriage, of sharing the same bed, this man should be accessible to her; yet he sat in his armchair, glowering fiercely down at some lawbook, as cold and stony and forbidding as when he passed sentence on a murderer.

At times like this, she was afraid of him.

Finally, she drew in a deep breath and said:

"All right, then, Henry. If you won't walk her, I will."

The judge muttered something beneath his breath and kept glaring at his open book. She could see the little muscles working at the corner of his jaw. She turned with an air of finality and went into the hall, thinking that she was as close to divorce as she'd ever been. The thought frightened her because of the way she accepted it—calmly, grimly, almost as an inevitability.

In the hall the overhead light had burned out. Resisting the impulse to go back to the living room and ask Henry to replace it, she fumbled in the closet in the dark and pulled out a heavy wool coat and her soft Russian-style fur hat. Her gloves lay on the small table next to the front door, by her purse and keys, and under the table were her rubber galoshes. She pulled on the boots and gloves, buttoned the coat, and turned to call Bitsy, their little black poodle, but the dog was already dancing in a tight circle around her feet. She attached the leash to its collar, checked its red sweater (she'd knitted it herself), then opened the door and stepped out into the darkness and snow.

Her resentment toward the judge built as she walked the dog. Lately their arguments had become long and bitter, starting over the least little thing and ending with days of burning stubborn silence. She felt she had lost her respect for him. He no longer seemed to care for her. She felt abandoned, alone.

He wouldn't even walk the dog, though he had done it himself for five years, every evening at ten o'clock, like a ritual.

The snow came to within two or three inches of the tops of her boots. The dog strained forward, tugging at its leash and heading for its favorite tree, the tall spruce at the rear of the house. At times she had walked the dog with her husband; normally, she watched from the bay window overlooking the side yard, while sipping her nightly cup of tea. Rituals. Perhaps, she thought, that had been their problem: too many rituals, not enough spontaneity. She shrugged, feeling the wind sting her face. Too late now for spontaneity.

It had quit snowing. The tiny black dog pulled her across the side yard to the huge evergreen. Funny, even their dog had developed unbreakable habits, emulating its owners. It always made for the tree, and left its offering of waste at the tree's edge where the bristling green branches dropped to within inches of the ground. Tonight the needles brushed the glistening white snow. The stars shone cold and sharp in a black sky.

Sometimes, she thought, standing in one spot as the dog did its little job, the judge acted as though he actually hated her. Was that possible? she asked herself. Was it possible for a husband to hate the woman he'd promised to love and cherish?

The wind made her shiver, even in the coat. As the poodle sniffed at what it had done, she realized that, in the darkness, she'd taken the judge's coat, quite similar to her own. It was too large and, like her marriage, fitted her uncomfortably.

Something rustled just behind her head, and she thought a branch of the tree must have brushed against her hat. Then there was the beginning of an explosion, but before she could comprehend it, the world seemed to explode and something blacker than the sky enveloped her.

Two

Kelso's telephone rang at 10:17 P.M. He lay on his couch in corduroy jeans, a cotton shirt, and a gray sweatshirt with a drawing of Sigmund Freud on the front. He was wearing heavy cotton socks and fleece-lined leather moccasins. The only light in the living room of his apartment came from the TV set. He was watching an old Sherlock Holmes movie, with Basil Rathbone and Nigel Bruce. His big yellow tomcat lay on his stomach, licking itself noisily and occasionally peering at him with grave greenish eyes.

Kelso reached out with one hand, found the TV remote control unit, muted the sound, and found and lifted the telephone receiver on the second ring. Since he was on call tonight, there was a chance it was Headquarters, but he hoped it was Susan Overstreet calling to say she didn't have to work late tonight after all and would be at his place shortly.

"Yes?"

"This is Meyer."

Kelso sat up, frowning. The cat made a low noise of displeasure and jumped off, onto the floor. Kelso felt a sense of irritation.

"Hello, Meyer," he said.

The small detective sergeant's voice was low and slightly sullen. "Homicide up on Wadding Way." He gave the address. "You're to get up there right away. Meet Smith."

"Are you going?" Kelso asked.

"Of course I'm going. I'm calling you, right? If I wasn't going, the dispatcher or somebody would be calling you. This is a biggie, some hotshot judge is involved. Hell, I wouldn't be surprised if Leill assigns the whole damn section to this one."

"Somebody murdered a judge?"

"Not the judge. His wife. We're wasting time, Kelso. Just get up there, okay? They'll fill you in at the scene."

"I'm on my way," Kelso muttered, and replaced the receiver.

He glanced at his watch. It was now ten-nineteen. He picked up his coffee mug and tossed down the last drops as the cat watched, looking resentful. He removed his moccasins and put on a pair of crepe-soled leather shoes, donned his parka and gloves, and checked to make sure he had his pipe and revolver. He always kept the .38 with him when on call.

On the TV screen, Holmes was peering into a window at some evil criminal. The game's afoot, Kelso thought, and clicked off the set.

"G'bye, cat," he said, and left the apartment.

George A. Kelso was a sergeant in the detective section of the Clairmont City Police Department. As of his last physical examination, seven months before, he had stood just under five ten and weighed 175—15 pounds too much, according to the doctor. This excess was mostly around his midsection, and came as the result of a highly select diet of pancakes, doughnuts, and other health foods. He carried a .38 Detective Special in a holster at his right hip and could be relied upon to use it, when absolutely necessary, with a rather high degree of accuracy. He was approaching the age of thirty-eight, beginning to worry about becoming forty, and watching his hairline slowly recede from his high forehead. His hair and his eyes were brown.

Driving toward the city from his apartment complex on the south side and waiting impatiently for the heat to come up in his old yellow VW Beetle, he listened to an oldies radio station that was playing "Come Go with Me" by the Del Vikings. As he drove, he thought about the judge and wondered which one it was.

Kelso was familiar with most of the city's judges, but personally acquainted with none. Listing them mentally, he tried to guess which might have a wife who would be a logical murder victim, but could not. Probably, he thought, it would turn out that the judge had killed her himself.

The night was cold and clear with a predicted morning low of seventeen degrees Fahrenheit. Only the main streets had been cleared of the recent six inches of new snow, atop the ice and slush left over from a couple of days ago.

It was Tuesday, January 12.

Wadding Way was in the northeast sector of the city, in one of the older and better neighborhoods. The people who lived here tended to be professionals, such as doctors, lawyers, and university professors, or else they were successful in business—banking, real estate, stores, and shops. You probably couldn't buy a house here for less than ninety thousand, and Kelso's city enjoyed a fairly low cost of living relative to larger places like New York, Chicago, or San Francisco.

The homes were large and impressive, with attached garages, tree-filled front lawns, and an atmosphere of wealth. There were no millionaires here; this was upper-middle America, possibly with a fringe of lower-upper. Some of the doors and windows still sported Christmas lights or wreaths, enhanced by the snow.

The tires of Kelso's VW hissed on the wet bare pavement; unlike lesser neighborhoods, this one had enough clout to warrant Department of Transportation plows. Kelso smiled wryly and braked the Bug to a halt near a snowbank, behind a couple of marked police cruisers and the crime lab van. Across the street were three more cruisers and two blue unmarked cars.

Meyer was right. Leill had probably called out the entire detective section.

One of the things that separated this area from the poorer streets was crowd reaction. Downtown or near downtown, any display of police authority would bring instant oglers; the area would have to be cordoned off.

Here, however, there was a marked absence of curiosity. Any watchers were behind heavy drapes, indoors and invisible. This was, above all, a *proper* neighborhood.

He climbed out of the car and felt the sting of cold air; he squinted at his watch in the light of a nearby streetlamp. Eleven o'clock. A sidewalk leading up to the imposing stone house had been shoveled and swept. A uniformed cop approached him along it, the collar of his wool uniform coat turned up, his cap visor pulled low over his eyes.

"Hello, Sergeant."

Kelso recognized him as one of the younger officers.

"Hello, Bieri. What's going on?"

Bieri grinned, but without much humor. "Judge Boller called it in himself. We found his wife out back, dead, lying in the snow. Bullet wound in the back of her head. Close range, according to the doc." He grinned again, rather slyly.

Kelso felt irritated. "What's so funny?"

Bieri shrugged. "Nothing, really. It's just the situation. See, there's fresh snow in the yard. She was popped at close range, but the only tracks are hers. And her dog's. Get it?"

"That's not so funny." Kelso glanced toward the front door, which had opened to emit Karl Smith, who stepped down from the porch and strode forward. Bieri's smile faded and he hurried away. Good, Kelso thought.

Detective Karl Smith was an imposing figure, over six feet in height. Additionally, he had the ability to intimidate many of the other cops with his sharp tongue and a rather clinical approach to things. Kelso liked him, but there were many who did not. Shivering, he watched the tall thin detective approach. In the darkness, his pale face was like a skull.

"I'm supposed to meet you," Kelso said.

Smith put a cigarette to his lips, puffed briefly, then took it away. He gazed at Kelso with icy blue eyes. "Looks like you succeeded, then."

"What's all this about a lady in the snow with no tracks but hers and some dog's?"

"God's honest truth, Kelso. Dr. Paul says she was shot at practically point-blank range, back of her head. See that tree?"

Kelso followed Smith's pointing thumb. The house occupied a corner lot, well back from the street, with the lawn extending around the front and side. Toward the rear corner of the lot stood a tall evergreen tree. The area around it had been roped off. Kelso could make out a dark form in the snow.

"Yes, I see it."

"Well, that's her, lying next to it. Apparently she was walking her dog. It's in the house now. Nasty little creature, one of those damned poodles, all skin and bones and a little fluff here and there. Why anybody'd want one is beyond me. Anyway, she'd taken it out for its nightly crap, according to the judge, when he heard a loud noise. Like a car backfiring, he actually said. He looked out and saw his wife lying in the snow and went out to her, but not all the way."

Kelso frowned. "What do you mean, not all the way?"

"He says he went only a few feet, just far enough to see that she was down and not moving. Then he ran back inside and telephoned an ambulance and us."

"That's interesting," Kelso said. "Why'd he call the police?"

"Says he realized the noise had been a gunshot. It's a terrible story, but so far he's sticking to it. And nobody's about to call Judge Henry Boller a liar, are they?"

"I don't suppose they are." Now Kelso remembered who Boller was: one of the sterner criminal court judges, feared by defendants and their attorneys for his harsh demeanor and severe sentences, and naturally admired and respected by prosecutors and cops as well as the so-called law-abiding public. "Are his footprints in the snow? Where he went partway toward his wife?"

Smith nodded, puffed at his cigarette, then tossed the

butt into the snow at the edge of the walk. ‘‘Don’t look like that, Kelso. There aren’t any ashtrays out here, are there? Yes, Boller’s footprints are in the snow, leading from the back door and stopping maybe a third of the way to his wife’s body, then returning to the door again. Just as he says. The only other tracks lead into the yard from the front door, right over there, and consist of his wife’s boots and the little holes their stupid dog made. We checked her boots against the tracks, and they’re a perfect match. So are the dog’s.’’

Kelso blinked. ‘‘How do you know about the dog’s?’’

‘‘We took it outside again, on the other side of the house, and let it prance around in the snow for a minute, and compared those tracks with the others. No, really, we did.’’

‘‘Okay. Well, I’m freezing. Let’s do something besides stand here.’’

‘‘What would you like to do?’’ Smith asked.

‘‘Talk to Judge Boller, I guess.’’ Kelso did not really want to interview Boller, but it would be necessary. It also would be quite touchy. The judge was an important person, the entire situation was extremely delicate; but the judge could not be ruled out as a suspect at this point. Kelso sighed and said: ‘‘Let’s go.’’

‘‘After you,’’ Smith replied with exaggerated politeness, and they went up the walk to the house.

Three

The front door was solid steel, but someone must have been watching from a window. As they approached the door it opened, and two uniformed cops ushered them into a long plushly carpeted hall as hushed and elegant as an expensive hotel.

"Kelso and Smith," Kelso said, not recognizing either cop.

"Yes, sir. Judge Boller's in there." The officer pointed at an opening a few feet along on the left.

"Thanks."

They entered a softly lit room with leather chairs and matching sofa, paneled walls, high ceiling, Oriental carpet, and a glass-enclosed bookcase along one wall. At the far end was a large stone fireplace.

Boller sat stiffly erect in an armchair turned toward the fire, his hands resting on the chair arms. He looked about fifty, very thin, with a narrow face, dark thick mustache, short dark hair combed straight back and graying at the sides. His eyes were narrow and black, his nose straight and sharp, his eyebrows black and heavy. He was frowning.

Hard, Kelso thought. Everything about the judge was hard, as if someone had built him of granite. The fingers gripping the chair arms were long and thin with well-manicured nails, and their tips pressed into the soft brown leather rather than resting on it gently. He reminded Kelso of a coiled spring; Kelso wondered if the dead woman had made the mistake of touching the spring's release mechanism.

If judges were supposed to be stern, he thought, then this one, Henry Boller, epitomized them.

Although it was after eleven at night, the judge wore a black vested suit, black shoes, crisp white shirt, and a silk tie with maroon and gray stripes. All he needed was a robe to sentence someone to death. Or perhaps just a Bible.

"Judge Boller?" Kelso said, softly and politely, and even that mild sound carried well in the quietness of the room. From somewhere he could hear the slow hollow ticking of a large clock. It was oppressive.

The judge's head turned, and the hard black eyes fastened on Kelso. Thin lips parted beneath the mustache.

"I'm Judge Boller." The words came low and harsh.

"Sergeant Kelso." He displayed his leather folder with the gold shield on one side and the I.D. card on the other. The judge nodded and Kelso put away the folder, adding: "And this is my partner, Detective Smith."

"Gentlemen." Boller made no effort to rise or to offer his hand, but merely nodded and frowned. Well, after all, Kelso decided, the man's just lost his wife, his mate of quite a few years has just been shot, he's probably in shock, or in a rage, or on the verge of a breakdown.

But Judge Boller didn't look near a breakdown; his eyes were black and shiny and alert.

"Do you mind if we ask you a few questions, your honor?"

"I've already answered questions tonight," Boller snapped, glaring briefly at Smith, then looking straight ahead again. His fingers dug into the supple leather armrests. "Well, go ahead. What do you want to know?"

"Can you tell us what time your wife left to walk the dog?" Kelso asked, taking out a small notebook and ballpoint pen. He unzipped his parka; it was hot in the room. Suddenly he was aware that he and Smith must have tracked snow onto the judge's immaculate carpet, but it was too late now.

"Yes," Boller said. "I can tell you that." The scowl never left his gaunt features. "It was precisely five minutes till ten, by that clock on the mantel."

A couple of logs blazed in the grate. On the mantel sat a

large round clock in a rectangular wooden case, with a white face and large black hands. It made no sound; the ticking must be coming from some other place in the house. Currently it read 11:17. Kelso held up his wrist; his own watch indicated 11:18, but it was normally a minute or two fast.

"It's quite accurate," the judge said severely.

Kelso nodded. "Yes, sir. So, at nine fifty-five she left with the dog. Would you just tell us in your own words—" Instantly he regretted saying it. Boller would probably think he was trying to imitate a prosecuting attorney examining a witness. And in whose words would the judge reply, if not in his own? He sighed and continued: "—what happened after that?"

Boller, staring directly ahead into the fire, replied in his low harsh tone: "Of course. Barbara went into the hall. The dog went to her. Bitsy is its name." He paused to clear his throat loudly; the sound echoed in the room. Then: "I heard the front door open and close, and went back to the book I'd been reading. After a few minutes I heard a loud noise. At first I took it for the backfire of some car or truck, but as I thought about it, I reckoned it might've been a gunshot. For some reason, I checked the clock again and saw that it was a minute past ten. At that point I got up and went to the bay window across the hall in the dining room, because it's got a view of the side yard that includes a portion of both the front and the rear. I couldn't see Barbara, but I saw the dog. It was running in circles, near the evergreen tree, dragging its leash."

"I see." Kelso made a note. "What'd you do then, sir?"

"I left the dining room and put on my boots, and went out—"

"Excuse me, your honor. Didn't you put on your coat?"

"No."

Kelso shrugged. "All right."

"I put on my boots and went outside, by way of the back door. That's in the kitchen, and it leads directly to the backyard. I've already told all this to several uniformed officers."

"Yes, sir."

"Something dark lay in the snow near the tree. I went a little ways toward it, about a third of the way, and recognized Barbara. She lay there, not moving, and I concluded that she'd been shot, so I ran back inside and called an ambulance and then the police. That would've been at approximately ten oh five."

"And you didn't go back outside after that, sir?"

Judge Boller's head moved almost imperceptibly left and right. "No. I did not."

"Your honor, this is probably a difficult question, but do you know any reason why someone would've wanted to kill your wife?"

Boller seemed to consider for a while, his black brows forming a deep V over his hawkish nose; then the long thin fingers left the chair arms and clasped themselves together over his vest, and he replied: "No. Absolutely no reason whatsoever."

Kelso sighed and glanced at Smith, who seemed to have gotten interested in some of the books behind the judge's glass-covered case, peering at them with his hands folded loosely behind his back like a browsing library patron, almost as if he weren't listening—except that Kelso knew Smith always listened, no matter what he appeared to be doing.

"Thanks, your honor," Kelso said. "I know this is difficult for you—"

"And yet," Judge Boller said suddenly, jerking his head around to scowl fiercely at Kelso, "that hardly matters, does it, Sergeant?"

"Sir?"

"My difficulties have nothing to do with it. This is a murder case, a homicide investigation, and you and your partner are the investigators. Isn't that right?"

"Yes, but—"

"My feelings in the matter are therefore irrelevant." As

if he were cutting off the objections of an attorney in court. "What *is* relevant, Sergeant, is that my wife's been murdered. You will therefore proceed to do whatever's necessary to find and arrest the person who did it, my difficulties notwithstanding. Don't you agree, Sergeant?"

"Of course, your honor. I was only—"

"Good." Scowling, he aimed his sharp gaze toward the bookcase, where Smith stood calmly regarding the judge with cold blue eyes.

"I've got a question or two," Smith said.

"Certainly," Boller said.

"Apparently your wife put on the wrong coat when she went to walk the dog. One of the uniformed officers says so."

Boller's chin jutted forward. "She made a mistake in the darkness."

"What darkness?"

"If you'll check—Detective Smith, is it?—you'll find that the overhead light at the front of the hall has burned out. My wife had to get her coat and hat from the closet in less than full light. Apparently she mistook my coat for hers. They're both similar, black wool and long, and we're almost the same weight and height."

Smith paced in front of the books, like a tall blond skeleton, then stopped and asked: "If you thought your wife had been shot, why'd you only go partway out to her? Why didn't you get out there as fast as possible and try to help her? You might've saved her life, for all you knew."

Kelso felt nervous, and looked to see if Boller was upset, but the judge blinked at Smith and replied evenly:

"I know nothing of emergency aid for a shooting victim. Besides, she wasn't moving. It wasn't up to me to move her, it was up to professionals. Also, on the chance someone had left tracks in the yard, I didn't want to disturb the snow." He paused. "*Were* there tracks?"

"Yes, sir," Smith said. "There sure were. I was thinking, though. If you already knew she'd been shot, especially if you thought she'd been killed, then you wouldn't have had any reason to go all the way out to her."

"What Smith means," Kelso put in quickly, "is—"

"What I mean," Smith said, "is maybe you aren't telling us the whole story."

Judge Boller stood up quickly and took a step forward. Smith watched him impassively, his eyes like ice under his heavy lids. For a moment they watched each other, their glances locked. Then, abruptly, the judge's features went sullen, his eyes narrowed, and he sank again into the leather armchair and seemed to examine his thin fingers.

"I'm tired," he said gruffly. "If you've any more questions, ask them. Otherwise, you're welcome to get out of my house."

"I don't think we've got anything else right now," Kelso said, putting away his pad and pen. He looked at Smith. "Ready?"

Smith shrugged. "Why not?"

They crossed to the hall door; the judge remained seated. At the doorway, Kelso paused to look back. "Excuse me, your honor. One other thing I just thought of. Did your wife always walk the dog?"

"It was walked every night," Boller said, his voice hard. "Just at ten."

"Yes, sir—but did *she* walk it? Or did you? Or did it vary?"

The judge gave him a long angry look and replied: "With few exceptions, I was the one who walked the dog."

"And," Kelso said, "while I'm thinking about it, did the dog follow any certain route? I mean, did it have a favorite tree or bush or anything?"

"It always went to the spruce tree in back," Boller said coldly.

"Thank you, sir."

"By the way," Smith said casually, "were you and your wife having some sort of argument tonight, before she left with the dog? Some kind of spat? Sex or money or anything?"

Boller stood up, his eyes flashing. "That's none of your damned business, Detective!"

Smith smiled. "What the hell, Judge, lots of guys fight with their wives. Do you own a weapon, by the way? A revolver or anything? Rifle?"

"I never have and I never will. They've already searched my house."

"Hmm. Too bad. Well, good night, Judge."

Boller muttered something Kelso didn't catch, and watched them leave. Out in the hall, as they zipped up their coats and pulled on their gloves, Smith chuckled.

"What were you trying to do?" Kelso asked. "What'd you want to go and get him all riled up like that for?"

"Just poking, trying to get a reaction," Smith said. "Come on, Kelso, don't be upset. He's only a damned judge, after all. He's only human."

"I suppose."

"Let's go have a look at the scene of the crime."

One of the uniformed cops opened the front door for them. When they stepped outside, the cold stung Kelso's cheeks and nose and made his eyes water. It was so clear that, even here in the suburbs, the sky was filled with stars. They went down two steps to the walk, then turned into the yard and headed out across the smooth snow-covered expanse in which Barbara Boller and her dog had left their footprints, toward the rear of the house. Large indentations from Mrs. Boller's rubber boots and smaller holes from the poodle's tiny paws formed a kind of zigzag trail toward the dog's nightly business and the woman's death. But they were the only tracks.

If a killer had been in the yard with Mrs. Boller, he had left no impression in the snow.

Four

The crime-scene investigators had finished, Dr. Paul from the Coroner's Office had made his initial examination, and the photographers had shot everything from a zillion angles. Some uniformed cops milled around the area, careful to stay off the actual site, and the ambulance attendants waited impatiently for the body.

Barbara Boller lay facedown in the snow, approximately two feet from the edge of the towering evergreen tree, ten feet from the white picket fence separating the backyard from a narrow cinder-covered alley, and fifteen feet from Agnes Street. She had short brownish gray hair, matted in back with blood. Her arms were out to the sides and her legs were together. She wore a long dark coat, black rubber boots, brown wool slacks, and brown leather gloves. A black fur hat, one of those Russian-style things, lay touching her hair where evidently it had fallen as she struck the ground.

The snow was covered with footprints all around her head, where all the different investigators had stood and knelt and peered, and Kelso could see the trail they'd left from her head toward the alley, and toward Agnes Street, and also back to the Boller house and the front street, Wadding Way. He glanced skyward and located the Big Dipper, then the North Star, something he'd learned from Susan Overstreet, who recently had gotten interested in astronomy. North was toward the alley; thus, Wadding Way ran east and west, Agnes ran north and south, and the house faced south. The dead woman lay by the tree, just at the intersection of Agnes Street and the alley.

Kelso wandered over to the wooden fence and peered down at the alley's cinder-covered surface, black between the snow-covered yards. Someone had plowed the alley, as well as the local streets. Influential neighborhood, he thought, when they could get even their back alleys cleared of snow.

He estimated the distance from the alley to Mrs. Boller's body and concluded that no gunman could have shot her from there. Besides, the wound was in the back of her head and she must have been looking toward the alley. The shot must have come from the opposite direction.

He went back and stood for a moment gazing down at the woman's body, then looked at Agnes Street, about fifteen feet away.

"The shot must've come from the side street," Smith said, as if reading Kelso's mind. "If she got it where she was standing, and fell forward without turning, then the bullet came from there." He jabbed a gloved thumb toward Agnes Street.

The reason all the investigators had walked and stood at the corpse's head was because her own footprints ran from her galoshes to the house, and everyone had wanted to avoid trampling on her tracks and those made by the dog. The woman lay like an inert toy connected to the house by a dark string stretched across the otherwise unbroken white snow.

"It doesn't make any sense," Kelso said. "Nobody could've shot her at point-blank range all the way from the street. Dr. Paul must be wrong, for once."

"Here he comes," Smith said. "Ask him."

Dr. Paul came toward them from the house. He wore an expensive leather coat, a hat bristling with black and brown fur, and supple leather gloves. His dress pants were stuffed into the high tops of polished leather boots. The Coroner's Office paid little, but already Paul had built up a nice private practice and was expected to resign his coroner's position soon.

"Hi there," Smith said. "You're just in time. Kelso thinks you don't know what you're talking about."

The doctor's intelligent brown eyes found Kelso. He smiled. "Really, Kelso? Did I get something wrong?"

"Smith's exaggerating," Kelso said, shooting a sideways look at the blond detective. "But we're confused about something. Are you sure the bullet was fired from close range?"

"Absolutely." Paul crouched over the woman's head. "The muzzle wasn't more than a few inches from her scalp. Look, you can even see singed hair."

"But there aren't any tracks in the snow behind her," Kelso pointed out. "See? Just hers and the dog's."

Dr. Paul stood up. "Well, I'll tell you definitely after the autopsy, but I'd bet money on close-range. Nearly point-blank."

"Well then," Smith said, smirking. "It's obvious what happened."

Kelso and Dr. Paul looked at him. Kelso said: "What?"

"The dog shot her," Smith said, and chuckled as he cupped his hands to light a cigarette.

The wind had come up and was blowing some of the snow. The branches of the evergreen waved gently. They all looked at the tree, which rose up darkly perhaps twelve feet into the night air.

"I've got it," Smith said. "The killer hid under that tree. Look. I'll prove it." He strode over to the evergreen and, with some difficulty, managed to part two of the lower branches and work his way between them. His height forced him to stoop. Once inside, he was clearly visible, standing just behind the limbs.

"You can come out now," Kelso said.

Smith spread the branches and emerged, frowning and brushing off snow that had gotten onto his coat and hair. "It was just a thought," he said.

"Even if it was possible to hide in there," Kelso said, "you couldn't have shot anyone out here at close range without coming out again, and the only tracks between her body and that tree are the ones you yourself just made."

Smith nodded, no longer smiling. "Yeah, you're right. I give up. So tell us how it was done, Kelso."

"Huh?"

"You always know how things were done. So quit trying to make me and the doctor look like fools, and tell us how it was done. How'd somebody get close enough to pop her at point-blank range in the back of her head, without leaving footprints in the snow?"

Smith often exhibited a strange sense of humor. Kelso assumed that this was one of those times. Shrugging, and starting to shiver from the cold, he shook his head. "How the hell do I know? I'm just as baffled as you are."

"I have a suggestion," Dr. Paul put in. "If you'd like to hear it."

"Tell us," Smith said, with mock enthusiasm.

"Well, it's only a suggestion. I'm no detective. But there were, after all, only one set of human tracks out here—those leading from the house to Mrs. Boller's body. You can't include the ones made by her husband, coming from the back door, because they never get here. But what if Judge Boller came out behind his wife and put his feet exactly where she'd already stepped, shot her, then went back the same way, walking backward?"

"Incredible," Smith exclaimed, rubbing his hands together and puffing hard at his cigarette, which bobbed at a corner of his mouth. "You've solved the whole thing for us!"

"Except," Kelso said, "that her tracks were checked, weren't they? You said they were a perfect match for her boots."

"Yeah." Smith was no longer enthused. "That's right. The crime-scene people checked. Yeah, forget that, Doc. They'd have found Boller's tracks superimposed on the ones from her boots. You can rule that out." He clapped his gloves together. "Damn, it's cold!"

"Well," Kelso said, feeling depressed, "either he shot her, or he didn't. And if he didn't, then . . ."

"Personally," Smith said, "I think he did. But is there any reason we've got to stand here slowly turning to ice? Nothing else is going to happen here. Let's give the medics the corpse and go someplace warm."

"Doughnuts and coffee," Kelso suggested.

Smith nodded. "Hot buttered Danish."

"Well," Dr. Paul said, "I've got to get back. See you, gentlemen."

Kelso heard a door slam and looked toward the house to see two men stepping down from the back porch and making their way across the snow, toward the body. The small thin black-coated one was Detective Sergeant Meyer; the plump youthful one was Stanley Broom. They approached, Meyer glaring and sullen, Broom faintly smiling. Meyer held out a plastic evidence bag.

"Here, Kelso. This is for you. I wondered where the hell you and Smith had gotten to."

"We were investigating the dog," Smith said, just to annoy Meyer. "We thought we'd collect its shit and have it analyzed by the crime lab."

"What?" Meyer scowled at him.

"Sure. See, my theory is, the dog did it. Nobody else's tracks are close to her body. So—"

"Shut the hell up," Meyer told him, and looked at Kelso again. "Here, Kelso. Take this."

"What is it?"

"A present from Santa. What do you *think* it is? It's the key."

"Huh?" Kelso stared at the bag. "What key?"

"*The* key," Meyer said irritably. "The one they found on the dead broad's body. Jesus, didn't they tell you anything?"

"Apparently not that."

"When the first cops got here," Meyer said, "they found her lying here in the snow, just like now, except that this key was on top of her body, right in the middle of her back, on her coat."

Kelso peered through the clear plastic. It was a small, plain, brass key. "Looks like a door key," he said. "There's a number on it. Two seventeen." He glanced up again. "Hotel room?"

Meyer shrugged his narrow shoulders. Next to him, Broom smiled, as though enjoying himself.

"Hotel, apartment, whatever," Meyer said. "Who the hell knows? It's got no name on it, other than the manufacturer. We'll have to try and trace it. Unfortunately, it's got no fingerprints."

"Surprise, surprise," Smith said.

Broom spoke for the first time: "We've just been inside, checking all the doors. Judge Boller claims not to recognize it, and it doesn't fit any locks in his house." Despite the cold, Broom wasn't shivering, and his voice came in its normal smooth tenor, pleasant and relaxed, as if he actually enjoyed standing outside in freezing weather in the snow late at night, over the corpse of a woman who'd been shot by someone who'd gotten very close to her without leaving a single footprint in the fresh snow and who, apparently, had left a key that fit no door.

Kelso sighed and held the bag out to Meyer, but the detective sergeant shook his head and said dourly:

"You keep it. Sign an evidence transfer slip, if you can find one. For your information, Leill has put me in charge of the investigation, and I'm assigning you to this key. I want everything you can find about it—who made it, who sold it, where it came from, where it's been, who had it last, and what that number on it means. You got that, Kelso?"

Kelso pocketed the plastic bag and shivered. "I've got it."

"Good. Broom and I'll check out the Bollers and attack the thing from that angle—domestic quarrel, secret lovers, that kind of thing. Okay, see you guys tomorrow morning. Come on, Broom."

"Certainly," Broom said, so pleasantly that Meyer shot him a hard look to see if it was sarcasm, but Broom only smiled warmly, and Meyer, scowling, looked away, muttering something under his breath. Kelso watched them cross the snowy yard to the front, climb inside a blue unmarked cruiser, and drive off down Wadding Way toward the business district.

"It beats me," Smith said, tossing his cigarette into the snow, "how Broom can stand to work with that little creep."

"I get the feeling Broom could work with the devil," Kelso said, quite seriously. Nothing seemed to faze Broom; he was like a big boat riding small waves.

"Come on," Smith said, sounding disgusted. "Let's go get some coffee. Or do you want to go home?"

"I'm not sleepy," Kelso said.

As they walked through the snow to the street, the medics were bundling Mrs. Boller into a yellow bag and hefting her into the ambulance. Kelso drove the VW toward the downtown area, huddling in his parka and waiting for the heat to come up. The streets were virtually deserted. A few of the brighter stars twinkled over the long line of streetlights and traffic signals. It was 11:22 P.M., Tuesday, the twelfth of January. The investigation had begun.

Five

Henry Boller sat before the fire, stiff and erect in his leather armchair, and gazed into the flames. Standing a few feet away, Detective Sergeant Meyer scowled at him, irritated by the man's attitude. This was a murder case, and it didn't matter one damned bit that Boller was an important judge with an unblemished record and the respect of the mayor and the city council. What mattered was that Boller was being uncooperative, and he, Meyer, had a job to do.

"I know it's late," Meyer said, unable to hide the sarcasm in his voice, "but I've been assigned to this case, and I've got a few more questions while everything's still fresh in your mind." He glanced sharply at Detective Broom, who seemed to find something funny, further increasing Meyer's sense of frustration. It was hot in the room. Meyer sweated in his heavy black overcoat. There was too much starch in his shirt—again. The stupid laundry never got anything right. He was a police detective, but apparently that cut no ice with those idiots.

"I've told you everything I can," Boller insisted, his voice low and hard. He kept his black eyes riveted on the flames.

"About this key," Meyer began, but the judge cut him off:

"I've already told you, young man, I know nothing about that key."

Detective Broom walked slowly toward the armchair and stood smiling down at the sharp-featured magistrate.

"Excuse me, your honor, but the reason we're confused is that the key doesn't fit any lock in this house, and we were wondering if your wife has a friend or relative who might've given her a spare key to their front door, for example. You know, friends do that, it's perfectly natural."

Judge Boller's head seemed to hunch farther down into the slump of his shoulders. The cagey old fart's hiding something, Meyer thought. Broom, as usual, was being far too nice—what was needed here was force, not diplomacy. That judge was no fool, he'd walk all over somebody like Broom.

Boller replied tightly: "Of course, it's natural. But it doesn't change the facts. And the facts are that I've never seen that key before tonight, I don't know anything about it, and my wife never mentioned such a key to me. Those are the facts." In the last sentence his voice trailed away into the hiss of the fire.

Lying bastard, Meyer decided. He glared at the judge's thin bony fingers gripping the leather armrests of his chair, the sharp small chin that jutted like that of a stubborn child caught in a lie, the beady black eyes whose heavy lids hung half-closed. With those black slow-lidded eyes and the jutting nose, he looked like one of those artist's renditions of a dinosaur. The judge is a dinosaur, Meyer thought morosely, a prehistoric bird left over from some long-gone age. And he's hiding something.

"Did your wife ever leave without telling you where she was going?" Meyer asked. "You think she ever tried cheating on you?"

Boller shot up from his chair and fastened his hard black gaze on Meyer, who took an involuntary step back. "Get out of my house," he snapped, "before I forget that you're supposed to be a policeman and that I'm a judge."

"We were just leaving," Broom said, with a vague smile. He put a plump hand on Meyer's arm and pulled him gently toward the hall. "Come on, we should—"

"Get away from me," Meyer told him. He hated being touched. He felt insulted. "Get off me." He scowled briefly at the judge, then followed Broom to the front door. They let themselves out and stood on the porch, buttoning their coats. Broom, half a head taller, smiled down at Meyer.

"I suppose you think it's funny," Meyer said. "Couldn't you see he was lying?"

"But you can't approach it that way," Broom replied. "You have to use a little finesse, you know. Boller's not going to respond to your usual tactics. There's no sense making him angry at you."

Meyer had never really understood Broom. Police work was relatively simple, in his view. You found the weak spots, then pressed hard. If you had the right guy, then sooner or later he caved in and confessed. "Finesse!" He spat out the word with disgust. "That's what's wrong with the Department these days. Don't you know what makes criminals tick, Broom? They know they can get away with it, that's what. You've got to show 'em they can't, pound them over the head, get tough, or the bastards'll eat you for lunch."

As they walked along the cement walk toward the cruiser parked on Wadding Way, Broom said: "So you really think Boller killed his wife?"

"Of course he did," Meyer snapped. "Who else could've? There weren't any other footprints in the snow, and she was shot at close range."

"There's no gun in Boller's house."

"That doesn't prove anything. He's hidden it somewhere, or gotten rid of it."

"But how'd he get close enough to shoot her? Without leaving his tracks in the snow?"

"I don't know." Meyer's head hurt and his nose was running. He felt miserable. He hated the judge and he was beginning to dislike Broom. "I don't know. But I'll find out."

"Well," Broom said, as they got inside the unmarked car and shut the doors, "it seems to me—"

"Can it," Meyer snapped. "Just can it. Look, it's

midnight. I don't want to think about it anymore till tomorrow. Okay?"

"Certainly," Broom replied, and settled back in the passenger seat.

Meyer steered the car toward Broom's apartment. He would drop the fat smiling idiot off, then go home and take a hot shower and hit the sack. Tomorrow he'd get up and things would be clearer. There had to be a simple explanation for the entire mess—the tracks in the snow, the key, everything—and tomorrow it would come to him, and then he'd show everybody how that judge had done it. Before anybody else could solve it. Especially before Kelso, who was developing a reputation around the detective section for being able to figure out the tough cases.

Boller did it, Meyer thought, gripping the wheel and glaring out at the snow-flanked streets. Boller's guilty as hell.

Head and eyes throbbing, he drove through the night.

Six

Only a couple of blocks south and a couple of blocks east of the Municipal Building was a pancake house Kelso liked, called simply "The Pancake House." Since it was en route to Smith's apartment, they went inside and ordered coffee and food—pancakes for Kelso, Danish for Smith.

"I thought you were only having a doughnut," Smith said.

"I was, but suddenly I'm starved. My God, I just remembered, I forgot to call Susan."

"You and she certainly have a strange relationship."

Kelso tapped out his pipe into an ashtray. "What do you mean?"

"Well, you're both too old to stay single, but all you do is date. On the other hand, sometimes you act married to her. What difference does it make whether you call her or not?"

"It's just something I do."

"Yes, but you seem to feel obligated."

Kelso felt embarrassed. "I don't *have* to call her."

"But you're afraid she'll be mad if you don't."

"I'd rather not discuss it, if you don't mind."

Smith shrugged and lit a Kent, then sipped black coffee.

"By the way," Kelso said, "if we're going to get personal, how come you're so concerned about your health that you refuse to eat meat, but on the other hand you smoke cigarettes?"

"You've made an error in logic," Smith said, smiling

blandly. "The one has nothing whatever to do with the other."

"They're both related to health, aren't they?"

"Not at all. My being a vegetarian is healthy, sure. But I smoke because I'm a hedonist." He chuckled. "Now, don't get all bent out of shape, Kelso. Let's talk about the case. Got any theories?"

"The dog did it," Kelso said, stirring sugar and cream into his coffee and scowling.

"Very funny."

A waitress brought their food and smiled as she set down the plates. She was tall and redheaded and knew both Kelso and Smith by sight, though presumably she didn't know their names. Kelso thought she was about twenty-two, with pale skin, freckles, and greenish brown eyes. Her grin revealed white straight teeth. Pinned to her waitress blouse was a plastic name tag with the word "Nikki."

"So what do you think," Smith said, eyeing the open V of her blouse. "You want to go out with me sometime?"

She grinned. "I've got a boyfriend."

"Oh yeah? What's he do?"

"He's in the Navy. Right now he's on an aircraft carrier over close to Japan."

"See?" Smith said. "No problem. What's your phone number?"

"It's unlisted," she told him, laughing. "Eat your roll like a good boy."

"I'm never a good boy," he said, and she went away.

"One day," Kelso said, pouring syrup over his cakes, "you'll be in here all alone, and three or four big burly Navy guys will come over and jerk you up from your booth and use you to swab the floor."

"Well, they'd better have a few marines with 'em, to help out."

"I don't think Boller shot his wife," Kelso said. He chewed pancakes, swallowed, and added: "Wouldn't he have thought up a different method?"

Smith blinked. "It looks like a very nice method to me, Kelso. He's engineered it so that it appears impossible for him to have done it."

"But there are too many questions. Boller's supposed to be a really bright man, from what I've heard. Have you ever testified in his courtroom? I have. He's sharp. Nothing gets past him. All the lawyers are afraid of him. If he was going to kill his wife, I think her body would've popped up way out in the country, maybe in another county, with no links to Boller at all. Not in plain view in his own backyard."

"Maybe he's even brighter than that," Smith suggested, "and he's pulling a reverse, shooting her in his own yard just so you'll reason exactly as you just did and rule him out."

"But what about that key?"

"Yeah." Smith nodded, bit off a huge section of Danish, and said: "That's the question, all right. That damned key."

"It's not polite to talk with your mouth full," Kelso said.

"Up yours, Kelso."

Kelso took the evidence bag from his jacket pocket and laid it on the table next to his plate. Through the plastic, the key was clearly visible—brass, with the name "ACE" in capital letters. He turned the bag over. On the opposite side was the number 217.

"Looks old," Smith observed.

"Yes." Kelso gazed at it while devouring the rest of his pancakes, from time to time adding extra syrup. Nikki returned with more coffee and left the check.

"Anything else, guys?"

"Nothing you'd care to sell," Smith said, smirking obscenely.

"Could I have a slice of apple pie to go?" Kelso asked.

"Sure thing."

"On top of *five pancakes,* Kelso?" Smith asked.

"It's for tomorrow," he said. "In case I don't get back here for lunch. It's homemade."

Nikki brought the pie in a Styrofoam container and Kelso asked:

"Excuse me, have you ever seen this before?"

She glanced at the plastic bag, then shook her head with a puzzled smile. "A key in a bag? No, I don't guess I have."

"Well, I meant the key. Know anyone whose apartment or house number is 217, and might've lost it?"

"No, actually I don't. Sorry." She raised her reddish eyebrows. "If you found it someplace, shouldn't you be turning it over to the police or something?"

Smith chuckled and Kelso said: "Yeah. Of course."

"Well, you guys come back, now."

"Tomorrow," Kelso said, adding sugar and cream to his fresh coffee, "we'll start checking all the key places. Maybe some local outfit makes Ace keys. And go from there, I guess."

"Sounds like great fun," Smith said.

Outside on the street it was bitterly cold, and the wind seemed to be blowing a few clouds in from the southwest. Kelso drove Smith to his apartment and let him out. Standing at the open passenger door, Smith peered into the Beetle and said:

"Don't pick me up in the morning, I'm taking the bus."

"Okay."

"It's better than freezing my ass in your car."

"What's the matter with your LTD?"

"It's in the garage for a new starter. Well, g'night. Hey, maybe you should go home and call Susan."

"Maybe you should turn blue."

Smith grinned. "I already have." He slammed the door and trotted up the steps to his building as Kelso drove away.

When he reached his own complex on the south side, it was after 1 A.M. His cat stretched and yawned, and he patted its huge head and fed it the smelly tuna stuff it liked. Recently he'd purchased an inexpensive answering machine; its red light was on, indicating a message. It was Susan:

"George, it's eleven-thirty and God knows where you are, but don't call me tonight. I'm going to bed and Aunt Eleanor's back home and she's got a bad cold. Call me tomorrow at St. Augustine and I'll buy you lunch. You can ogle the nurses. I love you. Over and out, or whatever. I hate this damn machine."

He smiled, undressed, and crawled into bed. The cat perched for a while on his stomach, kneading with its front paws, then got off and curled up against his legs. He fell asleep thinking about the key, and dreamed about a door marked "217." In the dream he used the key, but the door wouldn't open.

It was the end of the first day.

Seven

The telephone awakened her from some kind of terrible dream—the usual kind, in which she had become trapped in a cramped, enclosed space, unable to stand, the air growing hot and difficult to breathe, her screams becoming the jangle of the phone.

She rolled over, groaning, and grasped the receiver, brought it against her ear, keeping her eyes closed, breathing hard.

"Who is it?" Her voice came raspy with sleep.

"It's me," a man's voice said.

She listened, coming awake, focusing on what was happening. Over the telephone wires came a faint hum and a hint of far-off static, as though the call were long distance; yet she had the impression that it was not. A bad connection, from somewhere here in the city.

Besides, she knew him.

"What the hell do you want?" she asked. "Do you have any idea of the time?"

"Shut up and listen." His words sounded muffled, and she visualized him speaking through a towel. "There's been a problem. The police may talk to you."

"The police . . ."

She was awake now, alert, her body aching with the tension of the nightmare, shivering in the cold. By her bed the electric clock read 1:30. Her window was black except for the pale glow of a streetlight reflecting off the snow. The police, she thought, and frowned.

"Now, listen to me. If they come, you don't know me.

All right? You never met me. You never heard of me. You never had anything at all to do with me.''

Her mind was clear now, and she thought: Lying bastard. But above all else she was afraid of him. Cringing in the coldness of her bedroom and pulling the blanket up to her neck, she realized that she'd always been afraid of him.

''What do you want me to do?'' she asked, almost in a whisper.

''Nothing. Absolutely nothing. Just forget that I ever existed. Do you understand?''

Nodding, she replied hoarsely: ''I understand . . .''

''Good. Don't forget it.'' She heard a click, then the dial tone. With trembling fingers she replaced the receiver and reached automatically for her cigarettes and lighter. She smoked one down to the filter, huddled beneath her covers, staring at the pale rectangle of her window, then stabbed out the butt in the glass ashtray, buried her head in the pillow, and tried to sleep. After a few minutes she had to reach out and fumble for the Kleenex box and blot her eyes.

For over an hour she listened to the drone of traffic on the nearby highway, hating him.

Eight

The next day, Wednesday, January 13, Kelso arrived at the detective section on the third floor of the Municipal Building at ten minutes after eight, despite only five hours of sleep. Karl Smith was already at his desk sipping coffee from his plastic mug and reading a morning paper. Over by the windows, Broom bent over his desk blotter, smiling faintly as he wrote in a notebook. Meyer was nowhere to be seen.

Kelso went to his desk, squinting in the glare of the overhead fluorescent lights, which seemed even brighter than normal. The room reeked of tobacco smoke and the vaguely antiseptic odor of whatever the cleaning lady used on the floor. He sat down, put his revolver in a drawer, leaned back, and thought about the key. He pulled it from his pocket and put it on his blotter, still in the plastic bag.

The other detectives were at their desks: young Hawkins, who only recently had transferred to the section, and a balding middle-aged man named McNutt, with a round moon face, gold-rimmed glasses, and a paunch that made Kelso feel actually slim. Both were typing reports—Hawkins rapidly, McNutt hesitantly. From experience, Kelso knew that McNutt's result would be legible and correct; he wondered if Hawkins's speed included accuracy.

Leill's office door opened and the lieutenant peered out, his hard gray eyes darting around the duty room.

"Kelso. Come in here."

"Yes, sir." Kelso got up and crossed to his boss's office, glancing out the windows at the city. It had become completely overcast in just the past few minutes, and a few flakes of snow drifted downward. On the street, pedestrians walked bent against a sudden wind.

In the small office, Lieutenant Leill sat in a swivel chair behind a green metal desk. Everything in the office was institutional green. In the single window, the air conditioner had never been removed. Presumably it was now frozen. The lieutenant's gray eyes bored into Kelso.

"It's about the Boller case," Leill said.

Immediately, Kelso noticed something almost evasive about Leill's manner. His eyes seemed to falter at the last moment. He peered at his blotter. On his desk, in addition to the blotter, were a black telephone, a wooden pipe rack containing five pipes which no one had ever seen Leill smoke, a spotless amber ashtray, and one of those old-fashioned black penholders from which sprouted two black pens. Everything appeared recently dusted and unused. Leill leaned forward to rest his arms on the blotter and clasp his fingers, and the chair squeaked.

"You've been put in charge of the key that was found on Mrs. Boller's body, I believe?"

"Yes, that's right," Kelso replied.

The gray eyes flickered. "Well, I suppose you should continue that line of, uh, inquiry. But I'm going to add something to your duties in that regard."

Normally, Kelso remembered, Leill was direct, forceful, and to the point. Definitely, the man was hiding something.

"Yes, sir."

"I have reason to believe, Kelso, that Judge Boller shot his wife to death last night."

Silence, while Kelso considered this. The heat came on with a rushing noise. He felt the tug of warm air at the back of his head, since he stood almost directly under the overhead duct. He waited expectantly, unable to believe what Leill had said but ready to hear his reasons for it.

"This is an extremely sensitive situation, Kelso. Judge Boller's not merely a criminal court judge. He's an important man politically. There's even been talk of his running for office, possibly senator or representative. He has connections." Leill cleared his throat loudly. "Do you follow me so far, Kelso?"

"Yes, sir." Kelso kept his voice neutral. He thought: Cover-up.

"A man with that kind of political power, Kelso, is dangerous to cross. We've got to be careful. Cover our butts. However—" Leill frowned and lowered his voice. "He's guilty, as far as I'm concerned. So. Where does that leave you?"

Kelso waited. He felt awkward, standing almost at attention in front of Leill's desk. It reminded him of his Army days. He tensed. Evidently the lieutenant was about to order him to back away from the investigation.

"Kelso, Boller's a murderer, in my opinion. Is that door closed?"

"Yes, sir."

"This is confidential, Kelso. I got a call this morning. You don't need to know who it was, but I can tell you it was somebody way upstairs. You understand what I mean? Now, look: no damned politician's going to tell me how to run the detective section. As long as I'm in charge, I intend to do my job." He paused. "I want that judge, Kelso. I want him on a platter, all dressed and trussed and ready for the roasting oven. From this moment on, that's your number one priority, until you can make the arrest. Get that judge. He shot his wife, and I want you to prove it."

Kelso felt too stunned to know how to answer, so he merely said, "Yes, sir," and waited, feeling his palms sweating. Surreptitiously, he wiped them on the sides of his trousers.

Leill looked at him again with his intense gray eyes, and now there was no guile, no deception. "What about that key, Kelso? Anything on it yet?"

"No, not yet. I, uh, just started on it this morning."

"Well, get going, then. And remember—don't say anything about what I've just told you."

"No, sir. I won't."

"Good. That's all. I don't want to be disturbed."

"Yes, sir."

Kelso went out, closed Leill's door, and strolled across the duty room to his desk. The eyes of Smith, Broom, Hawkins, and McNutt watched him questioningly.

"He doesn't want to be disturbed," Kelso said, and sat down.

Smith said, "Ha," checked his .357, spun the cylinder, shoved the weapon into his shoulder holster, and added: "He's already disturbed."

"I'm going to make a few calls about the key," Kelso said, reaching for the telephone directory. "Then we've got to do some checking about the judge."

"Checking about the judge," Smith echoed. His ice-blue eyes hung just under his drooping eyelids, giving him a rather ghoulish appearance. "Is that what that was all about in there?"

"He just wants Boller checked out," Kelso said.

"Checked out, huh?" Smith grimaced. "I wonder if Leill was ever actually a detective."

Broom stood up and put on his coat. His plump pink-cheeked face was pleasant and his eyes sparkled with some secret humor. "Meyer and I are going to look into Mrs. Boller's background today," he announced, seeming very happy about it.

"Does that give you a big thrill?" Smith asked casually.

"Excuse me?"

"Looking into her background. A real treat?"

"Investigating is interesting work," Broom replied, still smiling, and left the room. He could be heard whistling softly as he went down the hall.

"Broom's a very strange person," Smith said.

Kelso was frowning at the yellow pages. "Did you know that there's no listing in here for keys?"

McNutt looked up. "You don't look under keys, Kelso. You look under locksmiths."

"Oh." Kelso flipped some pages. Under the heading "Locks & Locksmiths" was one company called Ace Locksmiths. There was no other Ace. Kelso lifted his receiver and punched buttons.

"Ace." It was a man's voice, fiftyish, bored.

"Sir, this is Sergeant Kelso at the police department, detective section."

"Police?"

"Yes, sir. I'd like to ask you a question."

"Well?"

"We've got a key with the name 'Ace' stamped on it. Could it be one of yours?"

"Describe it."

Kelso described it.

"Does it have a five-digit number, a serial number, on one side?"

"No, there's only a three-digit number, two one seven, like maybe a room number."

"Then," the man said, "it's probably a room number."

Kelso sighed. "Then you don't think it's one of yours?"

"Absolutely not. All ours've got a serial number, five digits and a letter. For instance, one six five three six B. It'd be like that."

"Well, thanks for your trouble."

"Did you wanta have it duplicated? We got special rates on duplication for law enforcement personnel."

"No thanks," Kelso replied, rather gruffly, and hung up. He sat glowering at the phone, then glanced at Smith. "Very funny. Special rates for duplicating keys for law enforcement personnel."

"Should've taken him up on it," Smith said blandly.

"Are you ready?"

"Ready for what?"

"To go check out Judge Boller."

"Right." Smith stood up, patted his shoulder holster, and put on his overcoat. He was wearing a dark blue suit and tie, light blue shirt, black shoes, tan overcoat—very natty. He put on a pair of amber-tinted aviator-style sunglasses and ran a thin hand through his light blond hair. "Ready."

Kelso slipped on his parka over his corduroy sports jacket, took the .38 from its drawer and put it in the holster at his right hip, zipped up the parka, shoved the plastic bag containing the key into a pocket, picked up his gloves, and headed for the door.

At their desks, McNutt and Hawkins continued to type, one slowly, the other rapid-fire.

Kelso and Smith went into the hall, down to the main floor, and out into the cold drab street, where the snow was beginning to fall harder and faster. According to a bank sign across the street, it was 8:40 A.M. and the temperature was thirty-one degrees Fahrenheit.

Nine

The logical place to start might have been the courts, which were located in the Municipal Building, but nothing really got going there until around nine-thirty or so. Prior to that, the attorneys and some of the judges tended to congregate in various coffee shops and restaurants in the area.

"Where're we going?" Smith asked, trying without success to keep the wind from mussing his hair.

"How about the Orange Tree?" Kelso suggested. They had to wait for a light at an intersection. A pedestrian in front of them ventured out against the DON'T WALK sign, and a motorist blared his horn and shouted something. The pedestrian, a young attractive female in dress and high heels, held up a finger at the motorist.

"Let's arrest her," Smith said.

"We have better things to do."

The wind whipped at their clothing and blew discarded paper along the gutters. "Anyway," Kelso said, "what about the Orange Tree? I remember hearing that Boller hangs out there from time to time."

"It's not even nine yet, Kelso. A little early for a judge, don't you think?"

"I hope so," Kelso replied. "I'd like to ask some questions about him, not run into him."

"Oh. Yeah."

The light changed and they started across the street.

"Hey, Kelso, look at that blonde over there. Nice little piece, huh? Look how she bounces."

"If you like that type."

"What type?"

"She looks a little cheap to me," Kelso said.

"Cheap? You're always putting me down, Kelso."

The Orange Tree was one of the newer places downtown, catering to the city's yuppies, or people who thought they were yuppies, by offering croissants for breakfast at inflated prices, and a variety of weird soups for lunch at inflated prices. Kelso and Smith entered, hung up their coats, and were seated in a booth by a grim-faced hostess in an orange skirt and blouse. She was between thirty-five and forty, overweight and flabby, and had actually dared to put orange-colored shadow on her eyelids. The result, Kelso decided, was comical, but he forced himself to say "Thank you" with a straight face, and she waddled away.

"I detest places like this," Smith said, glaring around at the orange booths and tables punctuated by huge artificial trees set in plastic planters. The floor consisted of orange-and-white-checked tiles, and there were garish orange curtains on the large plate-glass windows overlooking Third Street. The overall effect was rather overwhelming, or else disgusting—depending, Kelso thought, on one's point of view.

"What don't you like about it?" he asked innocently.

"It's like being buried alive inside a pumpkin. What's on the menu—orangeade?"

"They've got doughnuts," Kelso said, "with orange icing. And other things."

A young black-haired waitress in an orange skirt and blouse trotted over to their booth, opened her order pad, and smiled. She was overly made up, but otherwise rather pretty, with large dark eyes and a nice smile.

"I'll have coffee with cream, and a couple of glazed doughnuts," Kelso told her. "No icing."

"Yes, sir. And you, sir?"

"I'll have the orange duck," Smith said, eyeing her with a cold stare.

Her eyes widened and she blinked a couple of times. "Excuse me, sir?"

"Orange duck," he repeated, pronouncing it in exaggerated fashion.

"Sir, I'm afraid that's not on the menu."

"Not on the menu! Isn't this the Orange Tree? And you don't have orange duck? I want to see the manager immediately."

Kelso felt sorry for her. She seemed on the verge of tears.

"He's only kidding you a little," he said, glaring at Smith.

"No I'm not," Smith said angrily, then shrugged. "Oh, what the hell. Forget the orange duck. Give me a Danish. You *do* have Danish, don't you?"

"Yes, sir. Apple, cinnamon, peach, prune, and raspberry."

Smith jerked his head to stare. "What? No orange?"

"No, sir." The girl's voice came thin and breathless. "I'm sorry, sir."

"Make it apple, then," Smith said, and handed back the menu, looking glum. Then suddenly he smiled. "Say, how'd you like to have dinner with me tonight? You don't have a steady boyfriend, do you?"

The waitress blinked a couple of times, shot a helpless glance at Kelso, turned, and hurried away. Smith leaned back in his seat, lit a cigarette, and muttered: "Bah."

Five men in three-piece suits came in, talking and laughing loudly enough to be heard through the entire place, and settled into a large semicircular booth near the corner windows almost directly across the orange-and-white-checked aisle from Kelso and Smith. All five had spotless trenchcoats, which they hung on a rack near their booth; their short hair was neat, and their ties had subdued stripes and looked silk. They carried expensive-looking leather briefcases. It reminded Kelso of a fraternity party.

The frightened brunette brought coffee for Kelso and Smith, set it down quickly, avoiding their eyes, then retreated. A different waitress took the orders of the five well-dressed men; she was tall, poised, attractive, well built, with soft brown hair.

"I'll take that one," Smith said, ogling her.

"Sure you will," Kelso told him.

They sipped their coffee and listened to the conversation.

"I think I've got a cause of action against her," one of the well-dressed men said. *"Roland versus Westheimer's* being decided today. It's obvious that Roland is liable, but the real question's how much and what's the measure of damages. The trial judge completely screwed up the measure of damages, he used a prospective rather than a retrospective test. And not only that, he forgot all about the subjective and objective guidelines in the Central Industries case from last year."

"You're talking about Judge Brown," one of his companions said, lighting a long cigar. "He uses a prospective test for everything. Even when it's wrong."

"It's a matter of *res ipsa loquitur,"* a third man said. "That's hardly an outdated concept, you know. The tort law still recognizes *res ipsa,* and that's just what this case is. Negligence will be automatically inferred."

Smith leaned over the table and muttered in a low voice: "Lawyers." He looked disgusted.

Kelso nodded, trying vainly not to smell the cigar smoke. "Yes," he agreed. "Lawyers."

"Maybe we should ask to move to a nonsmoking section," Smith said, wrinkling his nose.

From the large booth came a fourth voice: "Did you guys hear about Judge Boller's wife?"

"No," Kelso said quickly. "Let's wait a minute." He pretended to search for something in his jacket pockets.

"Oh yeah, I heard this morning," a lawyer replied, not sounding very upset. "Too bad. Was it actually murder?"

"Well, I heard from a friend of mine in the prosecutor's office that she was shot in the back of the head with a pistol, right outside her house, walking her dog. In her own yard."

"No kidding. Who did it?"

"Nobody's been arrested yet. But I'll tell you something about Boller—"

"Hold it down, you want somebody to hear?"

The frightened young waitress came with the doughnuts and Danish and said in a loud high voice to Smith:

"Sir, I spoke to our manager—"

"Quiet," Smith snapped at her.

"—and he said he was sorry about the Danish—"

"Jesus," Smith told her, "I'm trying to . . ."

"And he says to tell you that next week we'll definitely have on our menu—"

"Can't you be *quiet?*"

"—orange Danish," she finished. She set down the plates and hurried away again, not looking back.

". . . his wife," one of the lawyers was saying. "But that's only a rumor, probably started by one of the other judges. Or some poor bastard Boller sent to the chair."

"I don't know," another lawyer said. "There's no law against a judge having an affair, is there?"

Instantly one of them asked in a low harsh voice: "Do we *have* to use that kind of language in a public place, for God's sake?"

There was a silence. All five well-dressed men seemed for the first time to notice that Smith and Kelso were close by in another booth. Kelso paid attention to his glazed doughnut and unfolded a newspaper he'd bought earlier. He handed Smith the women's section without cracking a smile, and let his eyes focus on an article about the Iran-Iraq situation while straining his ears for more talk from the lawyers. One of them said suddenly, loudly:

"So, anyway, in the Belcher case, it was the defendant's antecedent negligence, and not especially the issue of proximate cause, that the jury seemed to focus on. You know, I've never thought juries were capable of understanding proximate cause."

"All tort cases should be questions of law," someone said. "No tort case should ever be allowed to get to a jury. How the hell can jurors grasp complex issues like foreseeability of the risk or last clear chance?"

"But there'll always be questions of fact . . ."

Their voices droned on, with a forced quality, apparently now for the benefit of anyone listening. There was no more mention of Judge Boller.

"Finished?" Kelso asked, as Smith swallowed the last bite of his apple Danish.

"I suppose."

"Find anything interesting in there?" He indicated the women's section of the paper.

"Some nice bra ads."

"Well, well."

Smith left a tip—Kelso added to it, for the girl's frustration—and took the check to the cash register, where the grim-faced hostess did not smile one tiny bit as she took their money and handed back the change.

"Swell place you've got here," Smith told her enthusiastically.

Her sullen eyes, painted with orange shadow, regarded him dully. "Uh huh," she murmured.

"It's nice that you enjoy your work so much," Smith said. "By the way, do you pay much to get your eyes done that way?"

She looked confused and slightly irritated. Kelso bit his tongue.

"I don't pay," she said haughtily. "I do them myself."

"Oh," Smith said, grinning. "Then it's well worth the price." He chuckled as Kelso followed him out onto the street. Then he buttoned his coat and said: "What a bitch. How do they get any business at all?"

Kelso shrugged. "Lawyers seem to like it."

"I hate lawyers. So what do you think? Boller was having an affair? He had a mistress?"

"I think we should ask around. It's after nine now. Let's go see what's happening in criminal court."

"That Danish was stale," Smith said. "And overpriced."

"We'll have lunch at Hunter's, to make up for it."

The light turned to WALK and they hurried across the street and headed toward the Municipal Building. Snow fell heavily, and traffic was slowing as the streets turned white.

* * *

As they pushed through the revolving doors into the Municipal Building and waded through the usual throng of uniformed cops, attorneys, and secretaries, Kelso thought about Boller. If those lawyers in the Orange Tree had heard about a mistress or an affair, then it must not be exactly an ironclad secret. Others, also, must know. It should be a matter of asking the right people the right questions.

On the other hand, he could see two problems immediately. One, even if Boller had a mistress secreted away someplace, where did that get them in the investigation of Mrs. Boller's murder? Normally, in a love triangle, you could assume from the outset that either the cheating husband or his illicit girlfriend had killed the wife—but surely Henry Boller was incapable of such an act, despite what Leill seemed to think. Two, an affair proved nothing, even if it could be brought to light. It created suspicion, not proof.

They entered a crowded elevator and suddenly he thought, Yes, but what if Boller had a mistress, and what if that key fits her apartment door? What if Judge Boller was secretly seeing a woman whose address was 217 something?

And yet, why would the key to her house or apartment have been left behind on the dead woman's body? There were, he reflected glumly, many pitfalls in this case.

The elevator doors opened. Kelso and Smith stepped out into the fifth-floor hallway, turned left, and approached the criminal court division.

The floor was drab green tile. The walls were gray. Lining the wide corridor were green wooden benches on which sat a stratification of society, or at least of Clairmont City: men and women in clothes that were practically rags, their teeth yellowed and crooked, their hair disheveled, their eyes sunken with hopelessness or stupidity; respectable individuals in respectable clothes from Sears or J. C. Penney—clerks and truck drivers and repairmen and computer operators; farmers, recognizable by their craggy features, lined faces, weather-squinting eyes, bulging muscles and bellies, the men in baggy denims and plaids, or polyester trousers and brand-new dress shirts worn open at the collar, the women in silky print dresses or pantsuits and old-fashioned eyeglasses, their graying hair done up in tight little curls for ease of care; young punks and hoods, glaring, sullen and angry, at everyone, raw-boned and pale, or thin and black; and, finally, rich people, lawyers mostly, in tailored suits, shirts and ties from Redwood & Ross, salon-styled hair, gold watches and rings, and smiles of smug self-assurance.

Along one wall were several phone booths, mostly in use. On the opposite wall was a very high door, set off in carved paneling and bearing a small neat rectangle on which black capital letters read: CRIMINAL COURT.

Give us your poor, Kelso thought. Your huddled masses. He looked at the crowd and felt depressed.

He and Smith hurried past the people on benches, turned the corner at the far end, and went down a corridor with neither benches nor crowds. There was a door of normal size with a frosted glass window printed with black lettering: Criminal Court Office—Honorable Henry Boller. They went in.

On the other side of a long counter a bulky fiftyish woman sat at a green metal desk in an armless secretary's chair, frowning at a legal-sized document through bifocals attached to a black ribbon. Her thick-featured face was set in a grimace, her lips were bright red, and she puffed at a cigarette that dangled from one corner of her mouth. She had a huge bust. Thick flabby arms protruded from her short-sleeved dress. Her desk was covered with papers and documents; a ceramic ashtray overflowed with lipstick-smeared cigarette butts.

As Kelso and Smith approached the counter, she glanced up at them through the tops of her bifocals and asked in a deep gravelly voice:

"Help you?"

"Police, ma'am," Kelso said. "Is the judge in yet?"

"I know you," the woman rasped. "Kelso. Isn't that it? Sergeant Kelso. Detective section."

"Yes, ma'am."

"You testified in Judge Boller's courtroom two weeks ago, in that rape-murder case. The Elliston girl. I never forget a face."

"Yes, ma'am. Uh, this is my partner, Detective Smith."

"Smith." She peered at him. Ash fell from the cigarette as it bobbed in her lips. "You haven't testified in the judge's courtroom recently, have you?"

"Not in over a year."

"Huh. Well, I cut off my names and faces after a year. Too much clutter." She tapped the side of her head with a long, red-nailed finger. Her hair was thick and reddish brown, with hints of gray down under the surface. The overhead lights reflected in her glasses' lenses. "Well, the judge's not in yet. Is there any message? He's due in court at ten, so he'll be here in ten minutes." She held up a thick wrist and peered at a tiny silver watch. "At nine-thirty. Set your clock by 'im." She narrowed her eyes and asked, "About his wife's death, is it?"

"Yes, ma'am," Kelso said. "There are a few more questions we wanted to ask him. But it can wait. We've got some other people to see here in the building."

"Come back before nine-fifty if you want to see 'im," the woman said. "At ten till, he'll check over the docket, and be on the bench at ten sharp. And God help the poor schmuck who's late."

"Maybe we could ask *you* a question or two," Smith said.

Kelso cringed. Smith wasn't going to bring up the mistress thing, was he? With a secretary?

"I'll tell you what I can," she said. "My name's Florence Noonan, by the way. But don't ever call me 'Flo,' all right? And I obviously cannot and will not commit any breach of the judge's confidence. But otherwise you can ask me whatever you please."

"Thanks," Kelso said politely. "But we'll just be going—"

"What was Judge Boller's marriage like?" Smith asked. "Did they get along okay?"

It was so quiet in the office that Kelso could hear the huge woman's rasping breath, coinciding with the rise and fall of her massive breasts. Behind the bifocals her eyes seemed to bulge, and her bright lips turned downward at the corners. Damn it, Kelso thought, now we'll never get anything out of her.

The woman replied so softly that Kelso strained forward to hear.

"I'd never tell another living soul this. Except the police. And then, only because she was murdered." Florence Noonan paused, staring at Smith and breathing in and out, in and out. "He was meeting someone. Once a week, like a schedule. Don't ask me how I know. That's all I'll say. One evening a week, instead of going home. And I'd be here, finishing up some document or other, and the poor woman'd call. I'm talking about his wife, Mrs. Boller. And it'd be after seven or so, and I'd have to tell 'er that the judge was tied up late with a trial brief or a deposition or a conference in chambers. And the poor woman had to've known it was all a lie, because it was always on Thursday night, and she couldn't have been a fool. Every Thursday . . ."

There was a sudden metallic noise behind Kelso—the click of the door latch—and Florence Noonan's expression changed, her red lips curved upward into a tight hard smile, her thin penciled eyebrows raised over her bulging eyes, and she said in a loud, clear, gravelly voice: "Morning, Judge!"

Stepping back from the counter, Kelso and Smith turned to see Henry Boller entering the office, scowling with his fierce black eyes, dressed all in black—overcoat, suit, vest, tie, shoes—except for a crisp white shirt. His thin hawkish face jerked from Smith to Kelso to the secretary; then he stepped to a gate in the counter, pushed it open, and passed through to the other side.

"These gentlemen are police officers," the woman announced forcefully. "They've come to see you."

Judge Boller, as if recognizing them for the first time, halted in his tracks halfway to his own door, turned, and glared at the two detectives. In one thin hand he held the wooden handle of a black umbrella; in the other he grasped the leather handle of a large briefcase, old and battered and weighty.

"Why are you bothering me again?" he asked, his voice low and hard. "Didn't I answer all your questions already?"

"There are just a few other items," Kelso said. "Your honor."

Boller scowled at his watch. "Well, I can give you about five minutes. No more." He turned his back, stuck the umbrella under his other arm, opened his door, and entered his office, leaving the door ajar. His voice whipped out: "Send them in, Mrs. Noonan."

She nodded, her face expressionless. "You can go in now, gentlemen."

Already, as they went through the swinging wooden gate and crossed to the judge's office, Florence Noonan was once again frowning at her legal document, lighting another cigarette, and puffing hard, as if they were no longer there.

Kelso led the way. They stepped into Boller's office and closed the door behind them.

Ten

The judge was facing them at his desk, and now Kelso thought the man resembled a huge bird of prey, hunched over in his high-backed judicial chair, sharp shoulders raised, beak nose pointed at them, black brows arched over coal-lump eyes. Beneath the dark mustache his lips were a hard straight line.

The office was paneled on two walls; the other two were floor-to-ceiling shelves filled with lawbooks—Kelso recognized the state code, the Northeastern Reporter, and the state reporter. On the large old wooden desk were several opened volumes, a yellow legal pad partially filled with small neat writing in black ink, and a thick printed document.

Behind the judge, in a corner to the left of the bookshelves, was a small wooden door that, Kelso knew, led to the robing room and from there to the courtroom itself.

"Well?" Judge Boller's voice lashed out into the quiet of the small room.

A clock on a corner of the desk ticked like a time bomb. Kelso could not see its face.

"We were wondering, Judge," Smith said casually, as if he had ice water for blood. "Have you ever had any reason to believe that your wife wasn't being entirely faithful to you?"

Boller's face twitched at the corners of his thin mouth and he frowned harder and cleared his throat. "My wife—" he began, and coughed. "My wife could no more have been unfaithful to me than she could've immersed her bare arm in a vat of boiling oil. You'd have to have known her.

She was more than prudish; she was, let's say, *proper*. My wife was practically a Victorian.'' He started to add something else, then shook his head and waited, scowling.

''I see,'' Smith said pleasantly.

The judge glanced at Kelso. ''Anything else?''

''Did it go both ways, your honor?'' Kelso asked. ''I mean, were you as, uh, proper?''

''You people are barking up the wrong tree,'' Boller said coldly. ''You seem interested in finding some kind of sordid love triangle as the solution to my wife's murder. Well, I can tell you for a fact that there's no such triangle.'' He leaned back in the chair and began to rock slightly, so that the mechanism made a grating, squeaking noise, a kind of low counterrhythm to the rapid ticking of the clock on the desk.

''Sir—'' Kelso began, but the judge cut him off:

''Apparently you people have picked up some sort of rumor, some slanderous story. What you've got to remember is that judges, especially criminal judges, are vulnerable to that sort of tripe. Each week in this court I sentence men and women to prison, sometimes for life, occasionally without parole. Once in a while I sentence someone to death. I've no doubt that there are men and women out there who hate me enough to say anything, *anything*, about me. But I rise above it, and I advise you gentlemen to do likewise. Otherwise, you sink to their level, and you're lost.'' He stopped rocking and the squeak died. He stood abruptly and rested his thin hands on the desk. ''I'm due in court.''

''Sorry to have bothered you,'' Kelso said.

''Not at all.'' A veil slipped over the judge's eyes, a black screen that hid all thought or expression. He straightened and turned his back on them. The interview had ended. Kelso followed Smith out of the chamber, past the frowning secretary, and into the hall.

At the far end, a woman hurried around the corner and was gone.

Eleven

"Come on," Kelso said. He trotted down the hall, not waiting for Smith, who called after him: "What are you doing?"

Kelso had gotten a glimpse of a dark-haired woman in a white coat, tall and slender, with very short hair and a tiny waist. That was the overall impression. And she'd darted around the corner as if she'd been waiting or listening and, on catching sight of Kelso and Smith, had decided to avoid being seen.

In the back of Kelso's mind was an image of a third person, the paramour, the mysterious girlfriend whom the judge might or might not have been seeing in secret on Thursday nights.

Smith's shoes smacked the green tiles behind Kelso, and the detectives reached the corner at the same instant, turned it, and peered this way and that in the crowded corridoı. People had started filing through the tall wooden door into the courtroom.

"Did you see her?" Kelso asked.

"See who?"

"Dark-haired lady in a white coat, running around the corner just as we came out of Judge Boller's office."

"I didn't see anybody."

"She ran away. I think it could've been his girlfriend."

"Boller's?"

Kelso scowled around the area, at the green benches, at the courtroom door. He saw the ragged poor and the respectable middle-class and the important lawyers. Going to the door, he looked in at the courtroom, letting his eyes scan the spectators, the clerks, the attorneys at their tables near the bench, and a uniformed bailiff. There was no woman with a tiny waist, with dark hair, in a white coat.

"Hell with it," he muttered, coming back to Smith. "She got away."

"Did you forget to take your medication this morning, Kelso?" Smith patted his shoulder. "Remember, those pills are to keep you from hallucinating."

"Very funny. So you didn't see her and I did. It only proves which of us is more observant."

"Or less sane."

"Stop kidding around."

"Okay, okay, so you saw some broad making a run for it. Could've been anything."

"It could've been Boller's girlfriend."

They stood in the middle of the floor. Various people shoved past them, in a hurry.

"Why would she've run?" Smith asked. "After all, presumably she's never seen either of us before."

"Maybe she saw us go into his office," Kelso said. "Well, there's no reason to hang around here. I'm starving. What if we grab a bite to eat?" He started toward the elevators.

"I wouldn't want you to starve," Smith said.

On the ground floor they approached the revolving doors. A small dark scowling man in a dark coat came through, followed by a large plump smiling man. Meyer and Broom.

"Well, well," Meyer said, sneering. "Look what the dog pound left behind. What're you guys up to?"

"Get lost and then drop dead," Smith said, quite seriously.

"Hello, Broom," Kelso said.

Broom smiled and nodded. "Hi, George."

"We were just going for a bite to eat," Kelso said. "Care to come along?"

Meyer shrugged his narrow shoulders. "Why not? Broom and I've found out a few things you probably ought to know. I want a steak, but no place too crowded. No place with bad service. Nothing garish, I've got a headache. Nothing yuppie. I hate yuppies. Where're you guys headed?''

''The Orange Tree,'' Smith said, blinking at Meyer.

''We're going to Hunter's Restaurant,'' Kelso said.

Out on the street Meyer said emphatically: ''I'll drive.'' They piled into his unmarked blue cruiser. The snow fell harder, traffic was snarled, and the pavement was slick in spots, especially at intersections. It took twenty minutes to get to Hunter's, which was normally only a five- or ten-minute drive.

''Find out anything else about that key, Kelso?'' Meyer asked.

''Not yet.''

''What the hell've you been doing? Hiding in the toilet?''

''We were interrogating the judge,'' Smith said. ''And looking for mysterious women.''

''Oh yeah,'' Meyer replied. ''Mysterious women.''

They got out of the car and hurried into the restaurant. It was 10:30 A.M. and snowing hard.

Hunter's was at the east end of the downtown sector, and one of Kelso's favorite places. It was a plain-food restaurant, reminding him of a small-town coffee shop but with an urban atmosphere. The food was ''home cooking'' and wholesome, and not too expensive. Plate-glass windows overlooked Main Street, which over the years had become less than main as the Clairmont City business district gradually spread north and west. When founded a hundred years before, Hunter's had been at the hub of the tiny town of Mont Claire, which had become the city.

They sat down at a Formica-topped table, and one of Kelso's favorite waitresses, a busty blue-eyed blonde in her mid-twenties, came over to smile and hand out menus.

''Hello, Florine.''

''Hello, sir.''

Kelso could not prevent her from calling him that. He

ordered roast beef with mashed potatoes and apple cobbler, and she made him add green beans, "for his health." Smith ordered a vegetable plate. Meyer selected a New York steak, and Broom got a deluxe cheeseburger platter and chocolate malt.

"Say," Smith said, as the waitress went away, "her name's Florine. Isn't Boller's secretary named Florine?"

Kelso shook his head. "It's Florence Noonan."

"Well, maybe they're related."

"I talked to some people who knew Mrs. Boller," Meyer said, lighting a cigarette and loosening his tie. "Unfortunately, she's turning out to be as clean as a bar of soap. She didn't owe any money. She wasn't on any weird mailing lists, according to a friend of mine down at the post office. She only went out with her husband or a couple of lady friends. She even went to church, First Methodist, every Sunday morning. Without her husband."

"What's he?" Smith asked calmly. "An atheist?"

"Presbyterian," Meyer said, sounding slightly disgusted. "But he doesn't attend any services. Where was I? Oh yeah. Apparently she had no sex life."

"How'd you find out something like that?" Smith asked.

Meyer smirked. "I asked her lady friends. Just showed 'em my badge and said, 'Okay, this is an official police investigation, homicide. So tell me, did Mrs. Boller cheat on her husband? Did she sleep around? Did she have a hunk of meat on the side?' And they told me."

Kelso shook his head. "Did you use a little more tact than that, I hope?"

"Huh?"

"So she didn't sleep around," Smith said, sipping black coffee. "That doesn't help us."

"It rules out a lot of stuff, Smith," said Meyer. "A lot of motives. But I've got another theory."

"Tell us," Smith said.

"Boller sends guys up the river all the time. Not just that, but down the tubes, into the sewer. I know something about psychology, see?"

Smith groaned and Kelso chuckled to himself.

"I know how the judge's mind works," Meyer continued. "He's a tough guy, like an old-time cowboy in the Wild West. All around him is nothing but shit—people robbing, looting, murdering, stealing. Boller's got to try and control it. He's got to be tough."

"Just like Ronald Reagan." Broom said, with a shy smile.

Meyer shot him a glance. "Yeah. Well, anyway, Boller's fighting a losing battle, just like the rest of us, but he keeps on fighting. While other judges hand out mild slaps and the occasional spanking, Boller's dealing whips and chains. Right?"

"That's a brilliant exposition," Smith said, with great sarcasm, "but so what?"

"So here's what I figure." Meyer puffed at his cigarette and leaned forward. He looked like a small dark bird. "Somebody was blackmailing Boller, somebody who was about to go down the tubes, or the relative or friend of somebody like that. Whoever it was threatened Boller, using his wife. Get it? They told him to lay off of so-and-so, or his wife would die. Well, Boller, being a rock, ignored 'em, like any real hero would, and did what he had to. So the bastards killed his wife."

"What bastards?" Smith asked irritably. "What are you talking about?"

"I see what he means," Broom said. His smile was almost apologetic. "He means that some criminal defendant whom Judge Boller has recently sentenced severely, probably to life with no parole, or to death, threatened him with the death of his wife unless he reconsidered. At least, I believe that's what he means."

"Exactly." Meyer glanced at Broom. "Exactly. See, all we have to do now is check the court records and find out who Boller sent up for life or to the chair recently."

"And that's who shot Mrs. Boller?" Kelso asked.

"Somebody close to them shot her. Some friend or relative."

"Oh *well* then," Smith said. "That's all settled. The case is solved." He scowled at Meyer and muttered: "Jesus."

Florine brought their orders and for a while the talk stopped while everyone ate. Outside the windows, snow was beginning to accumulate along the sidewalks and gutters, and they could see it blowing across the pavement of Main Street. A salt truck rumbled by. The restaurant began to fill up with its weekday lunch crowd, and everything became a cacophony of dinnerware clanking, orders shouted to cooks, customers laughing and talking.

After a time, Kelso said glumly: "What we've got to do is find out where that key came from. And how she was shot by somebody who didn't leave footprints in the snow."

"By the way," Broom said, "the complete crime-scene report was brought up to the detective section this morning, and I read it over. There really weren't any footprints in the snow other than Mrs. Boller's and the little dog's, aside from the judge's tracks leading partway from the back door."

"How about on the other side of that fence?" Kelso asked.

"Exactly." Broom smiled. "They checked all that, George. No tracks on either side of the fence, along the alley, or along Agnes Street. At least, not in the snow."

"And yet," Smith said, "somebody got to her, held a gun to the back of her head, and pulled the trigger. It had to be Boller."

"Boller's footprints never got close to her body," Kelso pointed out.

"Nevertheless," Smith replied, "Boller's the only one who could've done it. You heard what Broom said, Kelso. No other tracks are in the snow."

"The murderer shot her from point-blank range," Kelso said, "and put a key on top of her body where she lay in the snow."

"It had to be Boller," Smith insisted.

"And," Broom said, as though pleased, "without leaving a single footprint in over six inches of unmarked snow."

"I think it was suicide." Meyer cut the last piece of steak into two bites. "She shot herself, tossed the gun into the snow, fell down, put that key on her back, and died."

"The dog did it," Smith said.

Kelso ate his apple cobbler and said nothing at all. But he didn't think it was suicide, and he didn't think Boller had done it. He ate his cobbler and sipped his coffee and thought about the dark-haired woman in the white coat. He wondered who she was. And he wondered if the number of her house or apartment was 217, and if the door could be unlocked using the key in the plastic evidence bag in the pocket of his coat.

Twelve

When all the plates were cleared away and they sat drinking coffee—except for Broom, who drank chocolate milk—Kelso told Meyer and Broom what Boller's secretary had said that morning.

Meyer smirked. "So the old fox sneaks out on Thursday nights, huh? Now we're getting someplace."

"How's that fit in with your blackmail theory?" Broom asked pleasantly.

"Huh?"

"Yeah," Smith said. "You think Boller was ready to send some guy to the chair, and the guy's friends shot Mrs. Boller. What's that got to do with an affair?"

"Forget the blackmail angle," Meyer said. "That was just one possibility. Look, if the old blowhard's been sneaking a little on the side every Thursday night, then there's our answer. Right? He's got some young broad lined up, he's tired of his old lady, he argues with her one night, she walks the dog, he holds a .38 to the back of 'er head, and blooey, no more old lady, hello young broad."

"He shot her himself?" Smith asked suspiciously.

"No," Meyer said. "He hired the chief of police to do it. Of course he shot 'er himself. He and his wife were the only people there last night, and there weren't any other footprints in the snow."

"Judge Boller's footprints weren't there either," Kelso pointed out, tamping tobacco into the bowl of his brier. Meyer watched, his small dark eyes sullen. Smith gazed out at the traffic and pedestrians along Main Street, where the snow had tapered off slightly but was blowing. Broom looked happy. "And," Kelso added, "there's the matter of that key. Boller wouldn't have shot his wife and left some kind of key on her body. He doesn't seem the type to play games with us."

"Maybe he didn't leave it there," Broom said. "Perhaps it dropped out of his pocket."

Meyer glared. "But it doesn't fit any lock in his house. Why would it've been in his pocket?"

They all arrived at the same answer at once, and Kelso said:

"His mistress." He told them about the woman in the white coat he'd seen hurrying around the corner outside Boller's office.

"So what we've got," Smith said, lighting a Kent and leaning back in his chair to cross his long legs under the table, "is this: Boller, a distinguished and hard-nosed judge, is tired of his marriage to a woman approximately his own age, and he's having some kind of passionate fling with a younger woman. Happens all the time. No problem there. What's he do? A cunning, shrewd, possibly even brilliant jurist, quite used to examining all sides of any question, he decides to murder his wife."

"Look—" Meyer said.

"Wait till I'm through, please. So, not only that, he decides to do it in a clumsy way."

"It wasn't clumsy," Meyer said. "She's dead."

Smith regarded him coldly. "I'm talking about the method. He makes her walk the dog—wasn't there something about that? Didn't Boller himself usually walk it? —anyway, she walks it, and somehow he gets to her without leaving his tracks, shoots her, drops a terribly incriminating piece of evidence on her body for us to find, and calls the police to report a murder. Then, when we arrive, he hands us some absurd story about hearing a backfire that he later decided was a gunshot, and admits going outside but claims he only went far enough to make certain she was dead, although how you can tell a person's dead by standing twenty-five feet away in the snow is more than I can comprehend.'' Smith's cold blue eyes rode up under his heavy lids. ''I just don't buy it. Not for a minute.''

''Well,'' Kelso said, ''there're other possibilities.''

Meyer glared. ''For example?''

''For example, Judge Boller didn't shoot her. His mistress did it. She wanted him for herself but Boller, being a prude, proper, Victorian, refused to divorce his wife. So his mistress decided to eliminate her. She found out Boller walked the dog every night around ten. She waited by the tree, and shot Mrs. Boller.''

''Hold on,'' Smith said. ''If she was after Mrs. Boller, what was she doing outside by the tree?''

''She saw Mrs. Boller come out the front door,'' Kelso said. ''Her original plan was to go inside and shoot the woman while Boller was out with the dog, but when she saw that it was Mrs. Boller, she hurried along to the tree. Then, after she shot her, she dropped her own key by accident—because of nerves, for example. There wasn't time to look for it, or maybe she didn't even realize she'd dropped it. She ran away, and there you are.''

Broom said: ''But I see problems with it, George. For instance, how'd the mistress do all this without leaving her footprints in the snow?''

''And another thing,'' Smith said. ''How'd she tell it was Mrs. Boller coming out, from a distance, in the dark?''

''Nothing's perfect,'' Kelso muttered. He lit his pipe, but it went out again promptly, leaving him sucking at air. ''What we've got to do is trace that key,'' he said, feeling depressed.

''We have to find out who the old bastard's mistress is,'' Meyer said. ''By the way, Kelso, I heard Leill called you into his office this morning. What'd he want?''

Kelso frowned. Either it was a murder investigation or it wasn't—he no longer felt inclined to keep secrets from people who were, after all, his partners. ''He thinks Boller's guilty," he said. "And he ordered me to prove it. He wants Boller on a platter, all done up like a duck ready for roasting."

"A duck?"

"Duck. Turkey. Whatever."

Smith said: "That sounds like Leill. What an asshole."

"Why's he so sure?" Meyer asked.

"He didn't say. But he seems awfully certain. Also, he hinted around that there was some kind of pressure from higher up, somebody wanting Boller left alone. But he said he was going to do his job anyway, and I'm to prove Boller guilty."

Smith chuckled. "Leill's having a little fun with you, Kelso. He's using psychology. See? The pressure from higher up is that somebody wants Boller's butt. But Leill knows you like to go against the political current, so he fed you the opposite story, just to turn you into a noble crusader. Now you've got a cause."

Kelso's face went warm. "Leill wouldn't try to manipulate me like that." But he knew it was quite possible.

"This is all bullshit," Meyer grumbled. "All that matters is who killed her, and no matter what politician's got his nose in it, our job's to find out. And we start with the key and the mistress."

"We'll take the mistress," Smith said, glancing at Kelso.

Meyer seemed about to argue, then shrugged his narrow shoulders and said: "Okay, Broom and I'll trace the key. Kelso, you still got it?"

"Right here." Kelso pulled the plastic bag from his pocket and handed it to Meyer. "You'll have to sign an evidence transfer form—"

"Later," the small detective sergeant snapped. "Later. Come on, let's get the hell out of here."

Outside on Main Street, very light snow fell and the wind was sharp. Passing cars threw slush onto the sidewalks. They found the unmarked cruiser and Meyer drove them across town again, to the Municipal Building. No one spoke.

When Kelso and Smith got out of the car and it had pulled away, Smith said:

"So where do we start? That secretary up in Boller's office?"

"It's the best place I know to start." Kelso was angry at himself. He realized that, until now, he hadn't really treated the case seriously. Despite the absence of tracks in the snow around the dead woman's body, he had felt it impossible for anyone but the judge to have shot her. The only problem had been how to prove him guilty. But now that there were other possibilities, he had to admit that Boller was only a suspect. It might have been the rumored mistress, or someone else entirely. And the key further complicated things.

From now on he'd have to approach the investigation with an open mind. And that meant not allowing people to evade questions. Just because Florence Noonan was the judge's secretary was no reason not to press her for answers. He felt grim.

They rode the elevator up to the fifth floor, made their way past the green benches outside the courtroom, strode down the side hall, and entered Boller's office.

Seated at her desk, Mrs. Noonan frowned up at them through the tops of her bifocals and said in her gritty voice:

"Oh, it's you two again. You'll have to come back later, I'm typing a document the judge needs right away."

"It'll only take a minute or two, ma'am," Kelso told her.

"Did you hear what I just said? I'm *busy*. Come back later." She bent over her machine.

Calmly, Smith pushed through the swinging door in the counter, stepped over to the woman's desk, reached out a long thin finger, and pressed the OFF switch on her typewriter. The clatter stopped. Florence Noonan jerked upright in her chair and glared.

"What do you *mean*—"

"Keep quiet and listen," Smith said, his eyes like ice

and his voice tight. ''When a police officer asks you to do something, especially in a homicide investigation, you do it. Understand? I don't care if you're the Queen of England. Now, who's this broad Judge Boller's been seeing on Thursday nights?''

Sometimes, Kelso thought, he and Smith were on the same wavelength. He suppressed a smile and waited for the secretary to answer.

Thirteen

"I've never been spoken to that way in my life," Florence Noonan said. Behind the thick lenses of her bifocals, her eyes bulged.

"Judge Boller's a suspect in a murder investigation," Smith said coldly. "You wouldn't want us to think you were hiding something, would you? Possibly covering up for him? There's such a thing as obstruction of justice, you know. You're familiar with the criminal law. You ever hear of accessory after the fact? Aiding and abetting?"

"Have you ever heard of slander?" she asked, seeming to regain some of her haughty composure.

"Ma'am," Kelso said, stepping up to the counter and resting his elbows on it, "all we need to know is the name of the person Judge Boller's been seeing on Thursday nights."

"I don't know her name," Mrs. Noonan snapped. "And even if I did know it, I wouldn't admit it. And in any event I'd never tell *you.*"

"I'm afraid, ma'am," Kelso said quietly, "you're going to have to come downstairs with us. To the detective section."

"You've got to be kidding!"

Kelso shook his head. He put his pipe in his mouth, but it had gone out again. He took it out and held it in one hand.

"No, ma'am, we're not kidding at all. Are we kidding, Smith?"

Smith's pale blue eyes never left the woman's face.

"We're not kidding even one tiny little bit," he said, his voice hard. At this angle, from where Kelso stood, he resembled an angry ghoul.

"I won't go," she said. But now a worried look had come into her wide-staring eyes.

"Then we'll use force," Smith said. Slowly, he grinned at her.

"All we want is her name," Kelso said. "Both of us are quite serious. You're withholding evidence. Nobody's going to back you up on a thing like this. Not even the chief of police, not even the mayor. If you want to try it, go ahead, but you'll only be disappointed. Not even Judge Boller would agree with you in this case."

"I'll call him," she said.

"Go ahead," Smith said.

She looked flustered. "This is an outrage!"

"What's her name?" Kelso asked. He was getting tired of it. Let's just take her down to the detective section, he thought.

Smith must have had the same idea. He said: "We've got little interrogation rooms down on the third floor. Just for people like you. Of course, you can call an attorney, but we'll get a court order, and you'll be given the choice of cooperating or being charged with complicity in a murder case." He shrugged. "It's up to you."

"What's her name?" Kelso said.

"Look," Smith said, "what the hell's wrong with you? What's it to you? Are you afraid of the judge? Don't you believe in anything, any kind of morality? If he's done something wrong, do you feel it's your duty to shield him? When his wife's murder's involved?"

"You could be shielding a killer," Kelso said.

Mrs. Noonan jerked her eyes toward Kelso. "You think the judge did it?"

"Nobody said that," Smith replied.

"But if you have information," Kelso told her, "and it's pertinent to our investigation, then you've got to tell us."

He thought Smith was about to add something, but suddenly the woman lost her nerve, or she decided it wasn't worth it, or she resolved some inner conflict. Her features softened, and now there was only fear and worry and a trace of resentment. She sighed heavily and frowned down at the keyboard of her typewriter.

"I only know the woman's first name. That won't get you anywhere."

Behind Kelso, the hall door opened. A pink-faced young man in a three-piece suit entered the office, carrying a briefcase in one hand and a sheaf of papers in the other. He blinked.

"I'd like to file—" he began, then saw Kelso and Smith, nodded politely, and said: "Excuse me, I'll wait."

"They were just leaving," Mrs. Noonan said. She pulled a long form out of her typewriter, rolled in a fresh sheet of paper, struck several keys rapidly, and jerked the sheet out again. She folded it like a letter, stuck it into a business envelope, and handed it to Smith, who put it in a pocket without looking at it.

"The information you requested," she told him, not meeting his gaze.

"Very kind of you," Smith replied. Grinning, he stepped over to the hall door and gave her a wave. "Take care, Mrs. Noonan. Give our regards to Henry."

Without waiting for any answer she might have had, Kelso followed Smith into the hall. Nobody was there.

"Come on," Kelso urged. "Let's see it. Open it up."

"Yeah, yeah, I can only move so fast, you know. I'm not Superman, despite opinions to the contrary."

"You really had her going in there."

"I was serious. The old battle-ax. I would've hauled her right down to one of those little rooms."

"Are you going to see what it says anytime today or tonight?"

"All right, all right. Here." Smith got the envelope open and unfolded the sheet of white paper. Florence

Noonan had typed one word, dead center, all in capital letters:

MARILYN

That was all.

"Great," Smith said. "So what do we do now?"

"Look for Marilyn, I suppose," Kelso replied glumly.

They went down the hall and turned the corner. Quite a few people still waited on the green benches or milled around the walls outside the courtroom, but Kelso saw no white-coated young woman with short dark hair. They took the stairs down to three and stopped off at the detective section to check for messages, but no one had called. McNutt sat at his desk, filling out a form. Hawkins had left. Leill's door was closed.

"Wait a minute," Kelso said. He opened his telephone white pages and looked up Noonan. There were several. He shut the directory.

"What was that for?" Smith asked.

"There's no Noonan whose address is 217 anything."

Smith nodded. "I already checked that, earlier this morning."

"Nice of you to tell me."

"You're welcome. I was thinking, Kelso. Today's Wednesday. Tomorrow's Thursday. Do you suppose the judge'll work late again tomorrow night?"

"I was wondering the same thing," Kelso said. He thought that their minds must still be on the same wavelength. "I don't know. So soon after the murder . . . but maybe it's worth a shot."

"We could tail him," Smith suggested. "See where he goes."

"In the meantime," Kelso said, "I'd like to talk to Judge Boller again and ask him point-blank if he knows a young woman named Marilyn. Just to get his reaction."

"He wouldn't react. And then he'd know we know about her."

"You're probably right."

"Let's ask around," Smith said. "You know any lawyers?"

"I know one named Raimy," Kelso replied. "J. Calvin Raimy. He's a defense attorney, I've seen him in Boller's courtroom. Usually Boller gives him a hard time, denies all his motions and petitions, overrules all his objections." He flipped through the yellow pages. "J. Calvin Raimy. His office is two blocks from here, on Fourth Street."

"Lawyers' Lane," Smith muttered. "Okay, let's go see him."

They put on their coats and gloves and went out.

Fourteen

The pink-faced young man in Judge Boller's office was a public defender who wanted to file a motion for withdrawal of his client's guilty plea. Florence Noonan already knew that Judge Boller would deny the motion; he despised public defenders. But she filed the motion anyway. As soon as the young man left, she got up from her chair and tapped on the judge's door.

It was his lunch break, and he wasn't due in court again until two that afternoon, when he would resume the trial of two men charged with rape. He would be in his chambers now, eating sandwiches from a brown bag and sipping black coffee from a thermos. She rapped again, feeling herself start to tremble.

His voice came loud and sharp: "Come in!"

She opened the door, peered around it, and entered.

"Excuse me . . . Judge Boller?"

He sat at his desk, in his black suit and tie and white shirt, glowering, part of a sandwich in one hand, a pen in the other. The mustache added to the gruffness of his features, which seemed pinched and sharp.

She thought about his wife.

"Yes?" He scowled up at her. "What is it, Mrs. Noonan?"

"A terrible thing's happened, Judge. I'm so sorry—"

"Don't whine, Mrs. Noonan. I've asked you not to whine. Just tell me what it is."

"It's about . . . Marilyn."

The expression on his face changed. Now there was

clearly something cautious, in addition to the irritability. A kind of awareness.

"What *about* Marilyn? For God's sake, close the door!"

"I'm sorry." Florence shut it, then faced him again. "Two detectives came, Judge. Investigating Mrs. Boller's . . ."

"Her murder. Get on with it."

She fought for control. "They made me tell them. I didn't want to, but they said I'd be an accessory, they wanted to take me down to the police floor, they said I was withholding evidence."

Judge Boller carefully set down the sandwich and pen, clasped his thin fingers in front of him on the desktop, and leaned back in his large leather judicial chair. She heard it squeaking over the ticking of the clock on his desk. He said, almost in a hiss:

"What exactly did you tell them, Mrs. Noonan?"

Her mouth went dry. Her eyes burned. I hate him, she thought. I hate him.

"What did you *tell* them?"

"I told them her name," she said. Her lips were dry; she licked them. She felt disgusted with herself, and she hated him.

Boller nodded and rocked. The chair squeaked. After a while he said, gruffly:

"There must be countless women named Marilyn."

She nodded and said nothing.

"Apparently you felt you had no choice."

She realized that she was afraid of him. "Yes, Judge."

"Please leave me alone now. I don't want to be disturbed. No calls, no visitors."

"Yes, Judge," she whispered, and backed out of his office.

She closed the door behind her, then leaned against it, trying to collect herself; her bifocals dangled from their black ribbon, rising and falling on her large chest as she breathed. Her temples pounded.

She went to her desk, found the aspirin in the middle

drawer, and swallowed two with 7-Up. I hate him, she thought.

The hall door opened. Mrs. Noonan looked up to see a tall young woman with thick black hair, cut short. She wore a long white coat, cinched at her tiny waist with a thin black belt.

The woman wore a huge pair of dark glasses, but Florence recognized her anyway, instantly.

Removing the glasses, the woman nodded and said softly: "Hello, Mrs. Noonan."

"Hello, Marilyn," Mrs. Noonan said.

Fifteen

The part of Fourth Street just east of the Municipal Building was referred to as "Lawyers' Lane" for the obvious reason that there were no fewer than seventeen law offices within a five-block stretch. They ranged along a continuum from a few prestigious, expensive, big-name firms, down through the modest and respectable, and ending with hole-in-the-wall places whose publicity was derived primarily from TV spots not unlike those for fly-by-night used-car dealers, stuffed in between segments of "The Barf from Mars." If you looked in the local bar association's monthly newsletter, you could identify these people and assign them to a slot. Either they were on the boards of various corporations and recipients of civic awards, or they were being reprimanded, suspended, or disbarred.

J. Calvin Raimy existed somewhere in the center of this spectrum. He was a well-known criminal-defense attorney, but there was something not quite reputable about him. He'd never been in real trouble, but rumor had it that all his dealings weren't strictly on the up-and-up. He was effective, though; if there was any chance at all of getting someone off, Raimy could usually do it.

Many of Raimy's clients sent him cards and letters from the state prison, but that could be said of most criminal lawyers. As Kelso well knew, the public perception of the penal system was backward; once caught up in the system, most criminals had a hard time avoiding incarceration.

Raimy's office was up a narrow flight of stairs in a creaking old building that years ago had been a hotel.

There was an elevator, but when its doors banged open, Smith took one look inside and stated flatly:

"No way, Kelso. You're not getting me in there."

Kelso looked and sniffed. The car was tiny and, from the odor, not ventilated. It reeked of cigar smoke, strong perfume, and, though it didn't seem possible, urine. Whatever it was or had been, he agreed with Smith.

"Let's take the stairs," he said.

On the second floor the hallway was almost too narrow for them to walk side by side. According to the street-floor directory, Raimy's office was number 22. They found it at the rear, where the overhead bulb had burned out and the hall was virtually dark.

"What the hell kind of clients can he possibly get in a place like this?" Smith muttered and rapped loudly on the door.

"I'd rather not think about it," Kelso replied. Law offices always depressed him. This one was already worse than usual, and he wasn't even inside yet.

The door was opened by a fat, balding, red-faced man smoking a thick black cigar. He stood just under six feet. At the back and sides of his head the hair was wispy and dark. He was thick-lipped and beady-eyed and wore a rather garish green suit, a red tie that had little green dots, and scuffed brown shoes.

"Yeah?" he asked.

"Mr. Raimy?" Kelso said, recognizing him.

"Probably."

"I'm Sergeant Kelso, and this is Detective Smith." He held up his I.D. folder. "Can you give us a few minutes?"

"I suppose." Raimy stepped back and ushered them inside, puffing hard at the cigar, which had the same sickening aroma as the elevator. They seemed to be in a kind of reception office, with cheaply paneled walls, faded brown carpet, three battered armchairs, and a low wooden table covered with old copies of *Time*, *People*, and *Newsweek*. Raimy faced them, puffing clouds of thick smoke.

"Whatever it is," he said, "I didn't do it." He smiled

slightly. "And if you can prove I did it, I plead insanity. What can I do for you, Officers?"

Kelso felt even more depressed. "We're investigating the murder of the wife of Judge Boller," he said glumly.

Raimy stopped smiling, but still looked faintly amused. "Oh yeah. The Boller thing. Heard about that. No arrests yet? What're you asking me about it for? Hell, I hardly knew the guy."

"What guy?" Smith asked.

"The judge. Boller."

"Did you know his wife?" Kelso asked.

"Not really. Met her once or twice, here or there. Not socially. Weren't you in Boller's court a few weeks ago, Sergeant Kelso? Testifying for the prosecution in the Manning case?"

Kelso nodded. "Yes. That was me."

"Got him off, didn't I? Despite your testimony."

"I seem to remember," Kelso said, keeping his temper, "that you made a deal with the prosecutor and entered a guilty plea to a lesser charge. Aggravated assault."

"Whatever," Raimy said, puffing vile smoke. "Anyway, I thought I recognized you."

"What about Judge Boller?" Smith said.

"Boller? You want my opinion? What a crass old bastard he is. My opinion, he's in tight with the governor, or one of the state supreme court justices, or some damn body, or else they'd have kicked his ass off the bench years ago."

"You don't especially like him, then," Smith said casually.

"Of course I don't like him. But so what? What's this got to do with his wife's murder?"

Kelso sighed. "What we'd like to know, Mr. Raimy, is whether you've heard anything lately about him. For example . . ."

"Is he sleeping with anyone in particular?" Smith asked.

The lawyer looked a little surprised. He took the cigar

out of his mouth and scrutinized it for a moment before answering:

"I've heard stories, here and there. What's this about, anyway?" Then he smiled. "Oh, I get it. Boller's wife's been murdered, and you're looking for a triangle. The old man might've had a mistress. Am I right?"

"You're quite perceptive," Smith said, straight-faced.

"My legal training." Raimy shoved the cigar back in his mouth. "They taught us to think logically and see all sides of an issue."

"My, my."

"You wouldn't have happened to've heard a name mentioned?" Kelso asked.

"No." Raimy shook his balding head. "But I heard a place mentioned." He smirked around the cigar, which he had worked to the middle of his mouth with his tongue.

"A place," Smith said. "And the place is . . ."

"Ever heard of the B & P?"

Kelso hadn't, but Smith said: "Sure. I've even been there, once or twice."

"Know what it stands for?" Raimy asked, smirking harder.

"I didn't know it stood for anything. Just letters."

"Wrong. I've heard it was for Bob and Paula, the couple who opened the place five, six years ago. Also heard it stood for bras and panties. And a guy told me it means bitches and pimps."

"That's all very interesting," Kelso put in, feeling uncomfortable, as though he'd mistakenly wandered into a stag party instead of the public library. "But all we wanted to know was whether you could tell us anything about someone Judge Boller might've been seeing. Other than his wife."

"That's what I've been telling you," Raimy said. "I don't know her name, but, as I was saying, several friends of mine have seen Boller at the B & P, from time to time."

"What's he do there?" Smith asked, deadly serious now. "Drink? Eat? Disappear into a back room? What?"

"I've never been there, myself," Raimy said, a little self-righteously. "Not my kind of place. As far as I know, it's just another dive—you know, a bar and some dancers. God knows what Boller does there. But if he had a girlfriend, I suppose he either took her there or met her there."

"Must've been quite a girl," Smith muttered.

Raimy glanced at his watch. "Well, I'm due in court, gentlemen. Was there anything else?"

"I think that about covers it," Kelso said. "Does the name 'Marilyn' ring any bells, by the way?"

"Marilyn. Marilyn." Raimy took his cigar out of his mouth again, looked at it, tapped ash onto the brown carpet, and returned it to his lips. "Nope. Can't say it does. Not the way you mean. Dated a girl named Marilyn once, but that was years ago, in my Navy days. San Diego. Redheaded girl."

"Thanks for your time," Smith said dryly. He and Kelso went to the door, then Smith turned. "By the way, that associate of yours . . ."

"I don't have an associate. I work alone."

"Oh." Smith nodded. "Just curious."

They used the stairs again. Back out on the street in the cold fresh air, Kelso thought he could still smell the cigar smoke and the stale urine-like odor that had seemed to pervade the entire building.

"What was that about an associate?" he asked.

Smith shrugged. "I thought I'd heard somewhere or other that he had one. I was just curious. Well, do you want to hit the B & P?"

"I suppose so," Kelso replied, without enthusiasm. "Tonight? Pick you up at seven?"

"Make it eight. We don't want to attract attention by being early."

"Maybe we should take dates."

Smith grimaced. "I don't think you take a date to a place like that, Kelso."

"Of course you do."

"No you don't. You go there to *find* a date. If you already *had* a date, you'd go someplace else."

Kelso frowned. They went back to the detective section, where he spent the remainder of the afternoon writing reports and otherwise catching up on paperwork. At five he got into his VW and drove home, feeling irritable and depressed. It was cloudy and cold and the forecast was for more snow before morning.

Sixteen

The woman was ushered into Boller's office, where he watched her unbutton her long white coat but not remove it. It was made of leather, soft and supple, and was one of the few things of which she was genuinely proud—she had managed to buy it with her own money. She sat in a visitor's chair and crossed her legs, watching the judge, who seemed, as usual, nervous and awkward. It was obvious that he disliked having her in his office—or, for that matter, in this building.

"I wish you'd called first," he told her. On his desk the pipes stood in their wooden holder, upright, polished, like new. The wind-up clock ticked loudly.

She controlled herself with an effort. "It doesn't do any good to call you," she said, keeping her voice low. "You never speak to me."

"I'm busy. I have work to do."

"Well, I'm here now."

"Yes." He frowned harder. With his stiff bristly mustache and bushy brows, he looked several years older than his actual age of fifty-one. "So what did you want?" he asked.

"I want to know what I'm supposed to do if the police . . ." She stopped, unable to find the right words. Besides, he knew exactly what she was talking about.

"I told you last night on the phone. You don't tell them anything. You don't know me."

"It'd be a good joke, wouldn't it, if they came here right now and found us together?"

Scowling, he said nothing, but his face reddened.

"I saw them earlier, in the hall," she said, taunting him. "They were coming out of your office, a tall blond one and a short one with sad eyes and a pipe. They were detectives, weren't they? I've seen them together, down on the police floors."

"You're not supposed to be hanging around here."

"I ran, before they could see me. Aren't you glad?"

He stood up behind the desk and narrowed his eyes. "You've got to leave. You can't stay here."

"Did you want me to tell them about us, Henry? About how you've used me all these years?"

"For God's sake, Marilyn . . ."

"You told me once, Henry, that if anything ever happened to Barbara, you'd marry me."

"That was a long time ago. Now would you please get out of here and leave me alone?"

"Was it a lie? Well, something did happen to her, didn't it?" She gave a short, involuntary laugh. Her fingers felt cold, despite the heat in the office. "Somebody put a bullet in her head. And we both know who it was, don't we, Henry?"

His face darkened like a thundercloud as he came around his desk and stood over her. She tensed, thinking he was going to hit her, but he only clenched his fists and glowered.

"If you don't get out of here, I'll call somebody and have you taken out by force."

She laughed. "Sure. Call the cops, Henry. There're a hell of a lot of things I'd like to tell them." She stood up. In her heels she was almost as tall as the judge. "Don't worry, *darling*. Remember when you used to call me that? I'll leave, you won't have to throw me out." Trembling, no longer smiling, she felt her chest filling with rage like an inflating balloon. If it bursts, she wondered, will I die? "Just remember one thing, Henry: the police *will* find me, I'm sure of that. And they *will* ask about you and Barbara—probably about us, too. And when they ask about us . . ."

Instead of finishing it, she turned and put a hand on the doorknob.

"Marilyn . . ."

"Yes?"

"Give me some time to adjust. After all, it was only a few hours ago. You can't expect me to recover from a shock like that overnight."

She nodded. The balloon opened, letting out some of its air, decreasing the pressure slightly. "All right, Henry. I'll give you a little time. I won't say anything. Yet." She opened the door and walked out of his office, not looking back.

Mrs. Noonan sat at her typewriter, but otherwise the outer office was empty. In the hall, a law clerk trotted along with a thick trial transcript and a Northeastern Reporter, but she didn't see any police detectives. She felt empty and cold, and wondered what she would do when the time came to make a decision.

Seventeen

When Kelso walked into his apartment that evening at a quarter to six, his telephone was ringing. He picked it up as the big yellow cat entered the kitchen, stretching and yawning.

"Hello?"

"George, it's me." It was Susan Overstreet. "Are you doing anything tonight for supper?"

"Just a sandwich."

"Aunt Eleanor's made a roast. Why don't you come over?"

"I would, but . . ." He looked at the large round clock on one wall. "I've got to go out again. Smith and I have to work."

"But you *have* to eat."

"Susan, by the time I got to your house, it'd be almost time to leave again. I'm picking him up at eight."

There was a long pause before she said in a subdued voice: "Are you avoiding me, George?"

"Of course not."

"How about stopping by later, then, when you're through? With Smith."

"When I'm through with Smith, or stop by with Smith?"

"I don't want to see him, I want to see you."

"It was just a joke." When she didn't reply, he sighed and said: "I'll see how it goes, okay?"

"I think we should talk, George."

"We have a date for tomorrow night, right?"

"I think we should talk tonight."

The problem was that Kelso was beginning to feel possessed. Owned. Locked in a room. He had no idea how to tell Susan about this without making her feel uneasy, or angry, or hurt. So he had been avoiding her. He didn't know what to do.

"I'll call you," he said. "I have to go now."

"I love you, George."

"Me too. G'bye."

He hung up first, rather than wait to see if she would. The actual problem, when he admitted it to himself, was that the relationship had progressed to the point at which the next logical stage was marriage, and Kelso had a terrible fear of marriage. For a moment he stood glaring at the wall phone, unable to understand why things like this happened. Everything had been so simple until the idea of a wedding had come up.

The cat whined. "Stupid cat." He patted its huge head and fed it the smelly tuna stuff it liked. He fixed himself a bologna sandwich, added four fig bars and a jelly doughnut, poured a glass of milk, and carried the whole thing into the living room, where he plopped down on the sofa, set the food on a low table, and switched on the TV.

Partway through the news, having finished the sandwich and fig bars, he decided that surely he'd missed something in the investigation of Mrs. Boller's murder. Muting the television sound, he began eating the doughnut. He thought about it, reviewing each detail in his mind. The cat came in, sat on the sofa next to him, and began licking its paws and face noisily.

Kelso pictured the Bollers' house before anything had happened, as if he were watching a play. It was almost 10 P.M., and on the ground lay six inches of fresh white snow, unmarked. Possibly the judge and his wife were arguing. The neighborhood, with its large expensive houses, was quiet. The latest storm had moved off to the northeast, leaving a cloudless sky, bright stars, and cold air.

The house sat on the northwest corner of Wadding Way and Agnes Street, facing Wadding, with an alley behind it.

At the junction of the alley and Agnes Street stood a tall evergreen tree. The back and side yards were separated from the alley and street by a white wooden fence.

The Bollers' front door opened. Kelso visualized a woman emerging, wearing a long dark coat and dark fur hat and rubber boots, holding a leash at the end of which pranced a tiny sweatered poodle.

The woman, Barbara Boller, stepped out into the six inches of new snow and walked her dog, leaving tracks from her boots and the dog's paws as they crossed the yard.

They turned north and went along the side of the house parallel to Agnes Street, making tracks in the snow, going toward the rear, and stopping near the tree.

Someone waited with a gun.

Where?

Someone appeared suddenly, materializing like a phantom or an alien in a horror movie, and stood directly behind Mrs. Boller—without making any impression in the snow.

Someone held the gun very close to the back of the woman's head and pulled the trigger.

Kelso winced. He saw the woman pitch forward into the snow, saw the leash fall from her gloved fingers, saw the poodle dash madly around her body, perhaps yapping. The entity with the gun disappeared in the blink of an eye, and then there was only Mrs. Boller's body and the dog.

A few minutes later the rear door opened and the judge appeared. He walked out across the unblemished snow and halted approximately a third of the way from the house to the tree. He regarded his wife's body, decided she'd been shot, turned, and retraced his steps to the door. He reentered the house and telephoned first the medics and then the police.

A third of the way to the body.

Shot at close range in the back of the head.

No footprints in the snow.

Kelso scowled at the TV screen, swallowed the last bite

of doughnut, chased it with milk, and leaned back against the cushions. What had he missed? He looked at the cat. Its big green eyes peered up at him.

"That's not the way it happened, old cat," he said.

The cat blinked, then began licking its hind feet.

Sometimes, Kelso wished he were a cat.

Eighteen

At two minutes to eight Kelso pulled up in front of Smith's apartment in his yellow VW Beetle and waited with the engine running. During the drive up from the south of town, the heat had come up, so at least it was warm in the car. The door of the building opened and Smith emerged wearing a long brown coat, brown fedora, and tan leather gloves. He strode down the cement walk, opened the VW's passenger door, and climbed awkwardly inside.

"You look like a German spy in a cold-war movie," Kelso said.

"Thanks. You look like a short dumpy cop with no taste in clothes. Or, for that matter, in cars."

"Why the weird hat and coat?" Kelso asked, pulling the VW away from the curb and heading into the near-northeast-side bar area.

"It's important not to look like a cop when you go to these places," Smith said.

The streets were clear, with dirty banks of snow piled at the curbs. The sky was a blotchy gray.

"I don't think I look like a cop," Kelso said. "What's this place like, anyway? You told that lawyer you'd been there a couple of times."

"I lied. That was just to win his confidence."

"Oh."

"I'd imagine it's like any other bar in this particular part of the city. Probably a lot of people laughing at the tops of their lungs and getting drunk. A very noisy and obnoxious band with amplified electronic junk music, and scantily clad wenches parading about on a stage."

"And of course you object strenuously to scantily clad wenches."

"I question their morality," Smith said. Then he added: "I don't mind looking at them, of course."

"Here we are." Kelso pulled the car into a slush-covered parking lot off the street. They got out, waded carefully to the sidewalk, and stood watching the entrance.

Everything was dark; the streetlamps seemed far apart. The buildings were brick, two- or three-storied, crowded closely together. Some were dark and apparently deserted; neon signs flickered over the doors of others, their colors reflecting in spots on the wet sidewalks.

Over the entrance to the place they wanted, red neon tubing spelled B & P, flashing on and off continuously. It looked to Kelso like an old ramshackle apartment building. The door opened, a man came out, turned, and helped a woman down two steps to the walk. He put an arm around her waist and began walking her toward the parking lot. He wore a suit and tie but no overcoat; she was in black spike heels, a short black dress, and some sort of fur thing over her shoulders, and held a small black purse. She giggled as he muttered something inaudible.

When they had passed out of earshot, Kelso looked at Smith and asked, "Did he take her there, or find her there?"

"Let's go inside," Smith said.

They stepped up to the entrance.

Inside, the first thing that assaulted Kelso was noise—loud and throbbing and amplified, just as Smith had predicted, emanating from drums, guitar, sax, and trumpet on a raised stage at the far end of a long room. The musicians, if you could call them that, were young men in faded jeans, black T-shirts, and black boots. Three had very long hair; the drummer's hair was shaved close to his scalp. The music was, Kelso thought, a form of rock.

The second assault came from the lighting. Colored

spots darted around the room, creating a constant flicker of blue, green, yellow, red, and violet, like the grand opening of a discount furniture outlet.

Along the right-hand wall ran a bar; only two stools were occupied. There were two bartenders, men in white shirts, both very busy.

To the left the bulk of the room was filled with small tables and, along the wall, wooden booths. A bouncer stood near the door, in dark slacks and a plaid sports jacket. He glanced their way with slitted eyes, then looked away, bored.

"I guess we just seat ourselves," Smith said, and led the way through the tables to a booth. Except for the strobing lights, it was very dark. They removed their overcoats and slid in opposite each other. "Look," Smith said. "Wenches."

He meant waitresses. Kelso saw two of them scurrying here and there among the tables, a blonde and a brunette, both young and attractive, wearing skimpy costumes with short skirts, mesh hose, heels, and plunging tops, all in black. Kelso stared long and hard at the brunette, but she was nothing like the woman he'd seen outside the judge's office.

The blonde came over to take their order.

"Evening, gentlemen. What can I get you?"

"Vodka martini," Smith said immediately. "On the rocks. Forget the olive. I hate olives."

"And you, sir?"

"Miller Lite," Kelso said. "And do you have food?"

"We order from the pizza place next door. I can get you a sandwich—you know, stroms, subs, like that. Or pizza."

"Half a stromboli, please," Kelso told her.

"Make it two," Smith said.

"It'll be about twenty minutes on the stroms. I'll bring your drinks."

"Is Marilyn here tonight?" Smith asked, very casually.

The blonde looked a little more closely at him. "Sure. You want me to give her a message or anything?"

"No, thanks. I'll talk to her myself." He ogled her chest. "Say, how do you keep that thing up with no straps?"

"It's a secret." She hurried away, smiling.

"Do you think the vice squad comes here often?" Kelso asked.

"Not so loud, you'll blow our cover."

Kelso shrugged. "Nobody can hear, anyway, over that music. So-called."

"I don't see any vice," Smith said, somewhat regretfully. "So, is that brunette the one you saw in the hall this morning?"

"No. By the way, what would you have done if the blonde's name had been Marilyn?"

Smith grinned. "Look at the check she left on the table."

It had been facing Smith. Kelso turned it toward him and saw that the waitress had left a check with their orders on it. In the upper right corner the name "Sheila" had been neatly printed.

"They do this in some bars around here," Smith said. "It's a copy. In case the customer later tries to claim he ordered something different."

"Oh."

The band stopped; the resulting silence was palpable. The trumpet player stepped up to a microphone.

"Ladies and gents, it's dance time. Let's have a warm welcome for Sweet Sugar!" He stepped back, there was scattered applause and someone whistled, then the band began a lilting Latin number. All the flashing lights went out, leaving a single red spot on the raised stage.

Into the spot strode a tall brunette in something resembling a red shortie nightgown and red spike heels. She stood motionless for a moment, then began to dance, slowly. There were a few calls of "All right!" and "Take it off!"

"So," Smith said, leaning closer to Kelso to be heard, "this is, in fact, a strip joint."

"She hasn't taken anything off yet," Kelso replied.

The blond waitress hurried over with their drinks. The music grew slightly louder, the beat heavier. The dancer was tall, slender, shapely, with a tiny waist. Her jet-black hair was short. Kelso sipped his beer, then leaned across the table.

"Smith."

"Yeah?"

"That's her."

"No kidding. Are you positive?"

"Of course I'm positive."

The music throbbed. Moving her hips sensuously, the dancer shed the outer garment, leaving red panties and bra. She kicked off the pumps and danced in her bare feet, teasing the audience by pretending to unfasten the bra. Eventually she did, her back to the tables, and let it fall to the stage. She turned quickly, slowly raising her arms over her head, as the crowd responded with a roar of approval and more calls and whistles.

The music built to a climax and the red spotlight winked out. When the array of multicolored lights flashed around the room again, the girl had gone.

Everyone clapped and a few customers called for more.

"Nice breasts, for a thin girl," Smith observed clinically. "But I'd rather see our waitress up there."

"You can't have everything," Kelso said. "Well, we've got to talk to her."

"Right. We'll cancel the food order and go find her. Probably there's a dressing room behind that stage."

"Let's eat first," Kelso said. He felt starved. "They might get suspicious if we canceled the order."

The band played another number, and their food arrived. Partway through the stromboli sandwiches, which were excellent, the red spot came on again and the trumpet player announced "Hot Spice," but this dancer turned out to be pale and overweight, with thick thighs and flabby arms, so that by the time she got around to taking off her top, there were more jeers and boos than applause. Someone yelled: "Get that blimp off the stage," and she turned without waiting for the band to finish and ran into the blackness behind the musicians.

Kelso found it quite embarrassing.

"You guys like anything else?" the blonde asked, returning once more.

"Uh, no thanks," Kelso told her. "We've got to see somebody."

Smith paid the bill, then asked: "Say, that dancer in the red outfit. Sweet Sugar?"

The waitress smiled. "You're in love with her, right? And you'd like her name and number. Or you want me to give her a message. Right?"

"Sure," Smith said. "How about it?"

Something flickered in the blonde's eyes.

"We already know her real name," Kelso said.

"Oh yeah. You asked about her earlier. Marilyn. Right?"

"Right," Smith said.

"Well, I'm not her pimp," the waitress said, frowning. "So deliver her your own damn messages." She trotted away.

Smith looked disgusted.

"Serves you right," Kelso told him. He slid out of the booth. "Come on, let's see if we can find her before they figure out who we are and warn her off."

"She's not her pimp," Smith muttered, and followed Kelso out across the floor. They held on to their coats and threaded their way between the tables toward the stage. As the band's blare became deafening, Kelso saw a closed door in a recess between the stage and the bar. One of the white-shirted bartenders gave them a curious glance.

"Rest rooms?" Kelso asked loudly, pointing toward the recess, and the bartender nodded.

Kelso opened the door and they found themselves in a narrow, dimly lit corridor. The music was reduced to a dull roar, punctuated by the boom of the bass drum. On the left were two doors marked GENTS and LADIES. At the far end was an emergency exit. To the right were two more doors, one marked OFFICE and the other simply PRIVATE.

"Let's try the private one first," Kelso said, and knocked hard, three times. The door opened inward a few inches. The brunette dancer peered out at them. Her eyes widened and she started to close the door, but Kelso shoved his bulk against it and said:

"Just a minute, please. Police. We'd like to talk to you."

Smith came up behind him, and they pushed their way inside.

Nineteen

It was a small dressing room, apparently converted from an office of some sort. A green metal filing cabinet stood against one wall, its top covered with dust. At the far end the door of a portable closet hung open, revealing a few articles of street clothing on wire hangers. There was a small dresser with bottles and jars and a large round mirror. Overhead, a bare bulb cast harsh shadows. There were no windows.

The girl stood in the center of the room, looking angry and frightened, then backed a few paces away as Kelso and Smith entered. She had put on the red brassiere, shortie nightgown, and pumps, indicating that she planned another dance before the evening's end.

Up close she looked older than she had onstage—somewhere in her mid-thirties, Kelso guessed. He saw dark circles under her eyes, as though from loss of sleep, and small lines at the corners of her mouth.

It was definitely the woman he'd seen in the corridor outside the criminal court.

"What the hell do you mean, barging in here like this?" she asked. Although she spoke loudly, Kelso detected a slight tremor in her voice and noticed her long pale fingers fiddling with each other.

"Sorry," he said, and showed his leather I.D. folder, giving her time to examine the gold shield on one side and the identity card containing his name and photo on the other side. He closed it and returned it to his pocket.

"Sergeant Kelso. And this is Detective Smith. We'd like to ask you a few questions."

"What is this, a raid? I haven't done anything wrong. The city ordinance says topless is okay. I didn't take anything else off."

"We're not vice cops," Smith said, a little irritably. "Do we *look* like vice cops?"

"What do you want, then?"

"Is your name Marilyn?" Kelso asked.

A different look came into her dark eyes—a kind of grim resignation, as of acceptance of something unpleasant.

"Marilyn Strauss." She edged her way over to the portable closet, reached inside, and rummaged around, keeping her eyes on Kelso and Smith. Kelso thought she was searching for a robe or a coat, but she brought out a pack of cigarettes, shook one up, pulled it out with her teeth, then stepped over to the dresser and started opening and closing drawers, frowning.

"Here," Kelso said, holding out his wooden matches. She gave him a strange look as he struck one and held it to the tip of her cigarette. Unlike some women, she did not use her hand to steady his. She puffed, and nodded.

"Thanks."

"You're welcome. Would you mind giving us your address, Miss Strauss?"

"I don't see . . ." She shrugged. "What the hell. It's 523 South Central Avenue. Apartment 3B. You want my phone number, too?"

"No thanks. It's not necessary." He took out a pad and pen and wrote down the address.

"So what's this about, anyway?"

"It's about Judge Boller," Kelso replied. "Did you hear about his wife?"

"I . . . I heard something about some judge's wife who got shot last night. Something about a shooting."

"It was Judge Boller's wife," Smith said. "You know him, don't you?"

Puffing hard at her cigarette, she sat down on a wooden

chair in front of the dresser, crossed one bare leg over the other, placed one arm over her thigh, and rested the other elbow on her knee, holding the cigarette near her lips, her black-shadowed eyelids lowered over eyes the color of semisweet chocolate. The sheer red nightgown was unfastened in front, exposing the tops of her breasts in the red bra, bare midriff, and smooth bare thighs. Although her waist was quite small, her hips were wide and her thighs were full. Kelso thought she wasn't bad-looking, despite the lines in her forehead and around her mouth; probably she'd been very attractive in her teens, like a prom queen.

"I asked you a question," Smith said.

Her eyelids fluttered, as if she had been daydreaming. "I'm sorry . . . what did you say?"

"I *said,* you know Judge Boller, don't you?"

"Well, I've heard of him. I guess I've read his name in the papers or something, or heard it on TV. It was his wife?"

"Barbara Boller," Kelso said. He thought there was something more here—she was hiding something, or she was afraid they would find something. It was a feeling he had. It reminded him of the old combination lock he'd had on a locker at school. He still had nightmares about it. If you turned it to the correct number but got it just the slightest bit off in one direction or the other, it refused to open. Very touchy. You had to get it exactly right. He thought Marilyn Strauss would be like that. She would require just the right touch.

"Barbara Boller," she repeated. She puffed at her cigarette, blew out a thin stream of smoke, and glanced from one to the other of them. Her voice was low, slightly husky. A very sexy prom queen, but fading now, like a photograph too long exposed to the light. "I'm sorry, I guess it just doesn't ring a bell."

"You were on the fifth floor of the Municipal Building this morning," Kelso told her mildly. He took out his pipe and held it between his finger and thumb, but didn't light it. "I saw you going down the hall leading from Judge

Boller's office. About nine-fifty or nine-fifty-five this morning. Remember?"

She blinked, tapped ash from her cigarette into a metal tray on the dresser, and appeared to concentrate, frowning slightly. "Nine-fifty-five this morning. I don't know. I could've been anywhere."

"But you weren't," Smith said. "Were you? You know damn well where you were, and it was in the corridor outside Boller's office. What were you doing there?"

She shrugged. "I don't remember being there, so how do I know what I was doing there?"

"You must remember," Smith said. "Kelso saw you. If he saw you, then you were there. Hell, we probably have a dozen witnesses who can put you there. As well as at the Boller house last night."

Kelso kept his expression bland, watching her face. She blinked again, hard, as if slapped, and frowned at Smith.

"At his house? You're out of your mind! I was never at his house."

"Don't lie to us, Miss Strauss," Smith snapped. "It *is* 'Miss,' isn't it?"

"None of your damn business."

"Everything about you is our business," Smith said. Suddenly he grinned and leaned against the closed door to the hall. He crossed his feet at his ankles, folded his arms over his chest, and said pleasantly: "You know, I wouldn't be a bit surprised if you're the one who shot Mrs. Boller. Do you own a gun? Or have access to one? Have you washed your hands recently? We can test your hands to see if you've recently fired a weapon, using various chemicals and ultraviolet lights. We can match your shoes and boots with the tracks we found in the snow, even though you didn't think we'd find any. Did you shoot her, Miss Strauss?"

Very deliberately, she crushed out her cigarette in the ashtray, then looked up at Smith. "I'm not stupid, you know. You guys are out of your heads. I wasn't there last night and you know it."

Kelso reflected that Smith had turned the combination dial too far. He had missed the exact number. The lock wasn't going to open now.

"All we know," Smith said, "is that you were at Boller's office this morning, right after his wife was shot, and now you're trying to deny it. In my book that makes you the number one suspect in a murder case. That means we're going to be watching everything you do, twenty-four hours a day, for the next week or month or year, whatever it takes, as long as it takes."

"How well do you know Judge Boller?" Kelso asked, keeping his voice level and polite. In a way, he felt sorry for her.

Her eyes met his. He felt close to the number again. She was going to tell him something.

"He's only a name," she said. "Like any other person in the news."

"Then," he said, "what were you doing up there this morning? Outside his office?"

She hesitated, staring. He was quite close now. She was trying to make up her mind.

"Look," he told her, conversationally, "it's not really a problem. We're just doing our job. You probably don't have anything at all to do with this, but don't you see that we've got to eliminate suspects? Why don't you help us eliminate you? Just tell me why you were there, and we can cross you off our list and be on our way."

"I was there . . ." Marilyn's chocolate eyes darted toward Smith once, then came back to Kelso. "I was there looking for my boyfriend. I heard he got arrested, and I was trying to find out about it. I asked in the office, but the secretary'd never heard of him." She sighed. "Somebody must've given me a bum steer. Apparently he wasn't arrested after all. So I left."

"What's your boyfriend's name?" Smith asked.

"Roy Welsh."

Kelso wrote down the name. "W-E-L-S-H?"

"Yes."

''Could you give us his address?''

''It's not 217 something, by any chance?'' Smith asked.

''Uh, I don't know his address.'' Marilyn hesitated, then added quickly: ''He comes here to the club, and after I get off work we go to my place. I've only been seeing him about two weeks. I just know he's got an apartment somewhere downtown. Not even an apartment, a rented room. He's not allowed to have guests.'' She grabbed another cigarette and Kelso again lit it for her. ''Thanks,'' she said.

''Let me get this straight,'' Smith said, no longer smiling. ''Some jerk named Roy Welsh comes here two weeks ago and gives you a story to the effect that he rents a room and can't have guests, so you take him home with you. And you hear he's been busted, but instead of calling the police to check it out, you go all the way down to the Municipal Building and then, rather than ask at the police desk, you go up to the criminal court office, though you have no idea if he's in jail or where the hell he is, and ask the secretary. And you expect us to believe that?''

She glanced at him, a dull look in her eyes. ''I don't give a damn *what* you believe.''

''We're going to check out this Roy Welsh,'' Smith told her. ''And we're going to check with Boller's secretary. And if you're lying about anything, we'll come back here and haul you downtown and put you in one of those little rooms and then you'll talk, Miss Strauss. Believe me, you'll talk.''

''Go to hell,'' she said, but without much conviction.

They were way past the correct number now. The lock wasn't going to budge.

Kelso stepped to the door and pulled it inward. ''Come on, Smith,'' he said glumly. ''Let's go.''

The open door let in the noise of the band.

''Another thing,'' Smith said, glaring at her. ''I don't care what the city ordinance says, in my opinion any woman who gets up in public and bares her breasts for a bunch of drunks is nothing but a common slut. Have you ever considered the immorality of what you're doing?"

"Oh yeah?" She stood up. "And you hated it, right? You hated it!"

"Aw, forget it," Smith muttered, and stalked out of the dressing room.

Kelso followed.

The door slammed shut.

Well, Kelso thought, so much for Marilyn.

Twenty

The hall was hot and stuffy. The band stopped, then launched into another number.

"Let's use the emergency exit," Smith said. "I don't think I can take that place again."

"It may be hooked up to an alarm," Kelso said.

"Who cares?"

Smith pressed the metal bar and the door opened, but no alarm sounded. They shrugged into their overcoats and went out. They were in a narrow alley between the backs of dark brick structures, the walls lined with trash cans, metal dumpsters, and packing crates. It was dark and cold, and snowing. Kelso smelled garbage.

"I'd say," Smith remarked, leading the way down the alley toward the street, "that we had a singularly unsuccessful evening."

Kelso zipped up his parka and pulled on his gloves, carefully stepping over the slippery bricks. "I'd say you were right, except for one thing."

"Yeah? What one thing?"

"She was lying. She went to see Judge Boller, it's obvious from the way she got so upset. She may as well've admitted the whole thing, for all the good it did her to deny it."

"Well, now that you mention it . . ."

"If you hadn't been so preoccupied with her breasts," Kelso pointed out, "you might've noticed her face and eyes and the tone of her voice. She was lying up one side and down the other."

"I wasn't preoccupied at all. It's just that girls who strip naked for pay have always irritated me. It's a question of morals."

"Which is the bigger sin?" Kelso asked, as they came out onto the street. "Topless dancing in a nightclub—or putting a bullet in the back of a woman's head while she walks her dog?"

"Obviously, topless dancing."

"So the point is—where's the stupid car? Oh, there it is—the point is, she lied. Which means she went to see Boller. Which means, taken together, that she's got something to hide. She's afraid of something, in other words."

They got into the VW and Kelso started it up. As they pulled away from the curb, Smith said: "That's an interesting point. Maybe she's afraid of Judge Boller."

"I think that's exactly what she's afraid of."

"Let's run her on the computer. Be interesting to see if we've got anything on her. And if she's got a weapon registered to her."

Kelso nodded. "We ought to run Roy Welsh, too."

When they were close to Smith's place, he said: "You want to come in for a beer or some coffee or something? A game of chess?"

"I'd like to, but I'd better call Susan." Kelso checked his watch by the glow of the dash. It was nine-thirty.

"Well, see you tomorrow, then," Smith said, opening his door as the VW stopped at the curb. "Kelso, what do you think, really?"

"I think Marilyn lied to us. I think she went to see Boller, and it's connected in some way or another to Mrs. Boller's murder. But I'm not sure about anything else."

"No, no, that's not what I meant. Do you think it's immoral, what she does in that club?"

"I think you worry too much," Kelso said, shaking his head in wonderment. "G'night, Smith." He started pulling away.

Smith tried to hold the door open, trotting alongside the car.

"Isn't it *immoral,* though? Would you want *Susan* doing that?"

"Good night, Smith." Kelso accelerated, leaving Smith behind. He reached across and slammed the passenger door. In the rearview mirror he saw the tall blond detective trudging up the steps of his apartment building, coat collar turned up, hat pulled low, shoulders slumped.

At this point, Kelso was twenty minutes from his apartment on the south side, and fifteen or twenty minutes from Susan's place on the northeast side. He pulled into a White Castle parking lot and used a pay phone on the corner. Snow fell in large puffy flakes, accumulating quickly. The receiver was cold against his ear.

"It's me," he said when she answered. "Can I still come over?"

"Where are you?"

"Downtown."

"Aunt Eleanor's kept some of the roast warm in the oven. Are you on your way here right now?"

"I'll be there in twenty minutes." He watched the snow drifting across the street. "Maybe twenty-five."

"See you soon."

He hung up, climbed back inside the VW, and drove northward, using his wipers every half minute or so.

As he drove, he thought about the case. Something was beginning to pester him in the back of his mind, like an insect crawling around in his brain. Dark-clad figure, he thought. Fur hat. Boots. Long coat. Mrs. Boller had taken her husband's coat by mistake, in the darkness of the hall. His coat was similar to hers. And she'd walked the dog, something Boller normally did himself each evening at ten.

It clicked suddenly, like a camera snapping a photograph, and he felt very stupid.

He found another phone booth and used it to call Smith.

"Were you in bed?"

"Don't be silly. I'm watching television."

"Is it any good?"

"It's a Hitchcock picture. *Psycho.* What's wrong, are you stuck in some ditch?"

"No. I've figured out something."

"Bravo," Smith said.

"It was staring us in the face all along."

"What was?"

"You remember," Kelso asked, "telling me that Boller always walked the dog at 10 P.M.?"

"Uh huh. That's what he said."

"And you recall that Mrs. Boller had taken her husband's coat by mistake, because a light had burned out and it was dark in the hall, and she could wear it because they were both the same size?"

"Yeah. So what's the point?"

"She was shot from behind."

"Kelso, is there some point? It's almost the shower scene."

"The point is, whoever did it wasn't trying to kill Mrs. Boller."

"That's very clever, Kelso. Of course, firing a bullet point-blank into a person's head can normally be expected to result in death."

"What I mean is, they weren't trying to kill *her*. They were trying to kill the judge. The killer thought it was her husband."

After a long pause, Smith replied in a different tone:

"Jesus, Kelso, I think you're right. It sounds obvious. Now."

"Yes. Well, I'll see you in the morning. I'm on my way over to Susan's. By the way."

"Yes?"

"I don't know how you can watch something as immoral as Janet Leigh cavorting nude in the shower."

He hung up before Smith could reply.

During the rest of the drive to Susan's house, he went over the crime again and again in his mind, and reached the same conclusion each time: someone had been trying to murder the judge.

When he arrived at the white frame house on the curving street in the dark quiet neighborhood, it was five minutes till ten, and snowing hard.

Twenty-one

Kelso could always tell when Susan's aunt wasn't in the house because the temperature was under eighty degrees, the level at which the old lady became warm. Lower than that, and she began to shiver. Kelso had never seen anything like it. It must have been only about seventy-five now, which meant Eleanor had been gone for half an hour or so. At least.

He removed his parka and gloves and sat down at the kitchen table opposite Susan, who had put chuck roast and vegetables on a platter and set places for two.

Susan Overstreet was seven years younger than Kelso and about three inches shorter, with thick blond hair, short and wavy, and dark brown eyes. It was all real, she was a natural brown-eyed blonde. Her slender build made her seem taller than she was. On this January evening she wore a red wool sweater, blue jeans, tennis shoes, gold earrings, and a gold bracelet. The collar of a white blouse protruded from the neck of the sweater.

Kelso piled meat, potatoes, and carrots onto his plate, poured coffee from the decanter, took a bite, and said:

"It's delicious. Aren't you having any?"

"I ate already. I'll have some dessert with you. So—what were you and Smith up to?"

"We went to a topless bar."

"Sure you did."

"No, really. We did. It's called the B & P and it's not too far from downtown, on the near northeast side. We went there to question a homicide suspect, and she turned out to be a topless dancer."

From long experience, Kelso could imagine almost exactly what Susan was thinking. She was picturing him in the bar, ogling the dancer, and growing slightly irritated. The irritation was being replaced by curiosity as to what the dancer looked like, and what Kelso had thought of her, and whether or not he had found her appealing.

"And you had Karl with you?" she asked, rather doubtfully.

"Of course."

"Karl Smith? The great prude of the world?"

"He's not a prude. He's just got a thing about nude dancers."

"And nude models, and nude centerfolds, bra ads—"

"So he's a little weird."

"How's the roast?"

"Great."

Susan had folded her arms across her chest and was frowning intently. "Why'd you watch her act, George? If you just went to question her, why didn't you just question her?"

"I didn't say we watched her act," Kelso said.

"Oh. Well, you didn't, then?"

"Actually, we did. But it wasn't on purpose. We were sitting there, and she just came out and started, you know, dancing . . ."

"What'd she take off?" She watched him suspiciously.

"Only her top."

"I see. And you looked?"

"What'd you expect me to do?"

"Hide your eyes."

Kelso sighed. "Well, Smith used his blindfold, but I'd forgotten to bring mine along. Now who's being a prude?"

She smiled faintly. "I never said I was a prude. I'm just curious."

Kelso sipped his coffee. After a while, Susan said:

"So, what'd she look like?"

"Tall. Brunette. Small waist. Very pale."

"How busty was she?"

"Just normal. I didn't take her measurements."

"Did she turn you on or anything?"

"I wasn't there to be turned on. She was a murder suspect. We went back to her dressing room, she had her clothes on, we asked her some questions. That's all."

"So she didn't turn you on?"

"As a matter of fact, she didn't."

He finished the meal and Susan took a chocolate pie from the refrigerator, freshly made that evening, with whipped cream on top rather than meringue, the way he liked it. She cut each of them a slice, poured more coffee, and sat down again across from him.

"So what's this murder case? Judge Boller's wife?"

"How'd you know?"

"It was all over the hospital today." Susan was a social worker in the psychiatric wing of a large downtown hospital. "Everybody kept asking me if you were assigned to the case. They seem to think it's really exciting or something. I suppose because he's a big-shot judge and has some money."

"Well, it's not exactly exciting, but it's kind of interesting." He told her about the absence of footprints in the snow, and the key they had found on top of Mrs. Boller's body.

"That's incredible, George. Do you think Dr. Paul's wrong?"

"I don't know. Probably not. We're waiting for the autopsy report."

"But suppose it turns out that she really was shot at point-blank range? What'll you do then?"

He shrugged. Actually, he had no idea what he would do in that case.

"You don't know anyone who lives at 217 something, do you?" he asked. "Anybody at your hospital? Maybe that med tech I caught fondling you in the cafeteria last week?"

"He wasn't fondling me, George. His hand was dangling over my shoulder, it was crowded in the booth." She grinned. "And I don't know anybody who lives at 217 anything."

They took their coffee in the living room. There was a small fire on the hearth. Kelso stirred it up and put on another log. They sat on the sofa, facing the flames, and she leaned against him, nestling her head against his neck. He smelled Chanel No. 5.

"This case is driving me crazy," he said after a while. "Nobody can walk on snow without leaving tracks."

"Maybe it was somebody in a balloon."

"Very funny."

"You need something to take your mind off of it, George."

"Like, doughnuts?"

"Don't be an asshole. Do I get a kiss?"

She got a kiss.

He left around midnight and drove through the city, which was cold and dark and quiet. The snow had stopped, leaving only about an inch of fresh covering. Traffic was at a minimum. He turned on the radio to the oldies station and hummed along with "Downtown" and "Kind of a Drag." As he was departing the deserted business district, the heat came up and his fingers and toes began to thaw.

At twenty minutes till one, he parked in front of his apartment, got out, went inside, and found his big yellow cat stretching and blinking in the entryway. He fed it, poured himself some milk, took a hot shower, and went to bed. Almost as soon as he closed his eyes, it seemed, the alarm clock sounded, and suddenly it was the morning of January 14, Thursday, the day on which Judge Boller had customarily "worked late" in order to see Marilyn Strauss.

Twenty-two

They sat around the long table in Conference Room 06-D, at 8:45 A.M. Meyer was at one end, scowling, smoking, hunched over in his black suit like a small dark bird. Broom sat at the other end, youthful and plump and smiling, bouncing a new pencil on its eraser. Smith sat across from Kelso on one long side of the table, smoking a Kent, his white eyebrows raised, looking unconcerned and a trifle bored. Kelso toyed with his pipe and from time to time sipped coffee from a mug.

It was a cold morning. The heat ran almost continuously, forming a low background purr. There were no windows.

"First thing is the key," Meyer said. "I worked on it yesterday, but so far it's a negative. We found the company that manufactured it, a place up in Chicago, but there's no serial number on it, so there's no record of its sale. Seems to be a pretty old key. The lab hasn't found anything on it except a few bits of lint that probably came from a man's white handkerchief. It's probably a door key, but the number 217 doesn't fit any door we've come up with."

Broom smiled and played with his unsharpened pencil. Smith puffed cigarette smoke into the air, gazing at the ceiling. Kelso sipped coffee.

"I understand that you and Smith picked up a possible lead, Kelso. You wanta fill us in on it?"

Kelso straightened himself in his chair. "It's not much. According to Boller's secretary—a woman named Florence Noonan—Boller's been staying late at the office on Thursday nights recently. At least, that's what he had Mrs. Noonan tell his wife. But in reality, she says, he goes off somewhere with a woman named Marilyn. And a lawyer named Raimy claims Boller spends time at a bar called the B & P. Smith and I went there last night and found a topless dancer named Marilyn Strauss, who claims not to know Boller and denies going to see him, but I think she was lying. We're having her run on the computer, along with some guy she says is her boyfriend.'' He shrugged. ''That's about it.''

''How about her address?'' Meyer snapped. ''Not 217 anything, is it?''

''Not the one she gave us,'' Kelso replied. ''And we haven't found an address yet for her boyfriend.''

''Work on it,'' Meyer said. ''We've got to hook this damned key up with something. It didn't materialize on that dead broad's back out of thin air.''

Smith glanced down the table at the detective sergeant. ''Really?''

''Shut up, Smith,'' Meyer said.

Smith grinned.

''I've been doing some research,'' Broom said suddenly in his mild voice. ''It's possible to search the city street index for certain addresses, on the central computer. I've asked them to find out how many 217s there are, and give me a list.''

Meyer raised his eyebrows. ''Now there's a son of a bitch who knows how to use his brains. All right, Broom. Let me know the minute you get something.''

''Yes,'' Broom said. ''I will.'' He smiled shyly and peered at his pencil.

''If that's it . . .'' Smith murmured, starting up from his chair.

''Let's hit it,'' Meyer said. ''We've got to wrap this thing up. Leill wants an arrest as quickly as possible. The mayor's giving him a lot of heat already. There could be a promotion in this for, uh, certain people . . .''

"Hooray," Smith said, got up, and left the conference room.

Kelso got up, too, tossed down the rest of his coffee, and pocketed his pipe. "I've got to go down to the computer room. Meyer, Broom—see you guys later."

"So long, George," Broom said.

Meyer nodded. "Get something, Kelso. Come up with something fast. We need to make a bust on this thing."

"Right," Kelso said, and went out and down the hall.

Cindy Raintree was in the computer office. Despite her name, she looked nothing like an American Indian. Or perhaps Kelso was wrong and Raintree wasn't an Indian name. Cindy was short, cute, bubbly, with collar-length orange-red hair and dark brown eyes. Since she was one of the Department's civilian employees, she wore no uniform. This morning found her in a brown and red pullover sweater, tweed skirt, and flats. Kelso noticed that the sweater was quite full of Cindy Raintree's chest.

"Hello, George." She beamed, her dark eyes sparkling. She always flirted with him, no matter how hard he attempted to discourage it. He supposed it was harmless.

"How are you?" he asked tentatively.

"Take me out sometime, and I'll show you."

"I've got a girlfriend."

"Not like me."

"Listen, I need some names run. Marilyn Strauss. Roy Welsh." He spelled them. "Strauss supposedly lives at 523 South Central Avenue, Apartment 3B. See if we've got anything on them, okay?"

"Will I get a present?"

"I'll buy you a cup of coffee."

"Karl Smith told me you were cheap. He was right."

"We're kind of in a hurry, Cindy, okay?"

"Susan Overstreet's not your type, George. I've seen her around. You need somebody more outgoing, perky, like me."

"As soon as possible. All right?"

She sighed. "Okay. I'll call you."

"Good."

He left and went up to the detective section, where Smith sat at his desk frowning at a notepad. Broom and Meyer had gone out. In fact, everyone else was out. Leill's door was closed.

"What are you doing?" Kelso asked.

"Looking at my notes and thinking. You know, Kelso, there's something weird about that setup."

"What setup?" Kelso went over to his desk and put on his parka.

"The Boller house. The dog. The tree. The backyard. The snow. I was thinking . . ."

Kelso tested the tobacco in his pipe with a thumb, then struck a wooden match and grazed the flame over the bowl, puffing a few times. He shook the match out and waited. When this happened to Smith, it was best to be quiet and let him proceed unprompted.

"If you wanted to kill Judge Boller, would you go to his house at ten o'clock on a cold night with fresh snow on the ground?"

Very nearly the same question had been in the back of Kelso's mind for some time—in fact, since waking up this morning. He hadn't phrased it quite as precisely as Smith just had, but it had bothered him.

"I'm not sure."

"Well," Smith said, "think about it. There's six new inches of snow. Now, unless you're a moron, you know damn well you'll leave tracks wherever you go. That's point one. You know, therefore, that as soon as you get to the judge's house, the only way to approach it is to leave your footprints in the snow for the police to find."

"Sounds logical to me," Kelso said. He unzipped his parka and sat down, puffing slowly at the pipe.

Smith leaned back in his chair, swiveled around to face Kelso, and narrowed his cold blue eyes thoughtfully. "But you go over there anyway. Fully intending to murder Judge Boller. Okay, now here's the second point. You take along with you a key. Not just any key, but a special key, one marked with the number 217. Knowing full well that, as soon as you've murdered the judge, you'll put the key right smack in the middle of his body, for all the world—including the police—to see. Got it so far?"

"Keep going," Kelso said.

"Fine. You get the picture? Here's some asshole with a gun, and a key, and he knows there's six inches of virgin snow, yet he plans to go over there and put a bullet in Boller's head and leave the key."

"Extremely intentional," Kelso said. "Extremely calculated."

"Ah." Smith pointed a long finger his way. "Exactly, Kelso. Calculated. This son of a bitch was calculating. He *planned* to leave the key, he *planned* to fire from point-blank range, he *planned* to do it with six inches of fresh snow in the yard . . ."

Kelso stood up suddenly and stared at Smith. "He planned for the snow. That means . . ."

It was quiet in the room. The only difference, Kelso thought, is a change of gender. She planned it, not he. Marilyn Strauss planned it. He took the pipe from his mouth; it had gone out. Placing it in his large ceramic ashtray, he rocked back and forth in his swivel chair, watching Smith.

"She'd already arranged some method of getting into the yard and getting out again, close enough to fire the gun an inch or so from Boller's head, close enough to put the key right on his body, but without leaving a single track in the snow."

"Yep." Smith sighed and opened a desk drawer. He took out his .357, checked it, put it in his shoulder holster, and stood up. He no longer had with him the long coat and felt hat of the previous night; he went over to a rack and lifted off a sheepskin coat. "The snow, or the absence of tracks in the snow, was planned. Just the way everything else was planned. The only thing the killer didn't plan on was Boller's wife being out there, instead of Boller himself."

"She must've known, probably from talking to Boller, that he walked the dog at the same time every night," Kelso said. "She must've known, in fact, that the tree was the dog's favorite place to go."

"Yeah, and . . ." Smith started to put on a pair of amber sunglasses, then paused. "Why do you keep saying 'she'?"

"Marilyn Strauss," Kelso replied. "Or have you forgotten about last night? You know—the topless slut?"

"Oh." He put on the glasses. "Well, I guess she could've done it, but frankly I don't think she has the brains to figure out something like this. I think we've got a fairly intelligent murderer on our hands."

Kelso patted the revolver at his hip, adjusted the zipper on his parka, and said: "By the way, now that you've figured out all that, what's the answer to the final question?"

"What final question?"

"Since everything was planned, how *did* the killer avoid leaving his, or her, tracks in the snow?"

"Damn, Kelso, I can't solve everything in one morning. I've got to leave something for you and the others."

"Generous of you. Come on."

"Where're we going?"

"I'd like another look at Boller's backyard. And I thought we'd check out Marilyn Strauss's apartment building, see what it looks like. Maybe there's a number 217. And I'd like a bite to eat."

"I figured you'd like a bite to eat."

As they stood in the hall waiting for an elevator, Smith said:

"You know, that blackmail angle Meyer was talking about earlier, I've been wondering about it. Do you suppose it would hurt to check the court records and just see if Boller's recently sentenced anyone to death with a 217 address?"

"I don't suppose it'd hurt," Kelso replied, without much enthusiasm. "I don't suppose it'd help much, either, if you want my honest opinion."

"Nevertheless," Smith said, "I think I'd like to try it."

An elevator opened, but before they could get on, Judge Boller stepped out into the corridor and frowned at Kelso. His face looked gaunt and pale behind the thick dark mustache.

"Sergeant Kelso," he said gruffly.

"Your honor," Kelso said politely.

"I see you're leaving. Do you have a minute, before you go?" Boller hesitated, glanced at Smith, then looked at Kelso again and added: "Alone?"

"Sure," Kelso said.

Smith shrugged. "I'll go down to the computer room for a while."

Kelso led the judge back into the duty room, took off his parka, pulled up a wooden chair for Boller, and asked: "What's it about, your honor?"

Boller's black eyes looked sunken, as if from lack of sleep. Glancing once around the large room at the empty desks, as if to reassure himself that no one else was present, he said:

"It's about Marilyn Strauss."

Twenty-three

The morning sun slanted in through the windows on the long wall of the detective section duty room, casting long shadows from the desks and chairs. Kelso sat sideways at his desk, his back to the windows, so that Judge Boller, facing him, had to squint. The venetian blinds had been raised for the winter, to provide the fullest possible warmth, and the low-riding sun beamed directly into the judge's eyes, forcing him to peer into the glare in order to meet Kelso's gaze, rendering his expression more fierce than normal.

"Yes, sir," Kelso said, his voice absolutely bland. "Marilyn Strauss." It was rather like an interrogation in one of those old crime movies, he reflected, with harsh light being aimed into a hapless suspect's eyes. On the other hand, it had its disadvantage—with Boller squinting like this, it was virtually impossible to read his face.

"What you have to understand, Sergeant—" The judge paused to clear his throat loudly, then continued: "What you have to understand is that for the past ten, fifteen years of my marriage, my wife and I didn't have a normal physical relationship. Do you understand what I'm trying to say?"

"Yes," Kelso replied. Where had he heard this before?

"To put it bluntly, we didn't have sex."

Kelso nodded. He folded his hands across his slightly round belly and waited, frowning, wondering if the judge had come to give him useful information or complain about his wife.

"Are you married, Sergeant?"

"No."

"Have you ever been?"

"No."

"Well, try to imagine it. A great deal's said and written about marriage these days. When I was a young man in law school, people were always talking about marriage as if it were one continuous fling. I had quite a, what you would call, a libido, in those days. So did my wife." He glanced down at his hands, which were thin and white with very black hair on the wrists and tops of his fingers; then he squinted up again. "After a few years, Barbara lost interest in the bedroom, except for sleeping. At first I blamed myself, then I stopped. It was nothing to do with me. I put it to her clearly: either things would have to change, or I'd have to find some other outlet for my needs."

Kelso nodded carefully. Boller was obviously leading up to an apology for having slept with Marilyn Strauss. He wondered why the judge was bothering about it. Why should he care what the police thought about his affair? Unless, of course, he had shot his wife.

Or, Kelso suddenly realized, unless Boller knew that his wife had been shot by Marilyn Strauss.

"Maybe I'm not making myself clear," Judge Boller said, scowling into the sun. "Let me put it this way. I had a minor affair here and there, along the way, the same as many men in my position. You don't believe it? You think high office renders you immune from bodily needs? Well, believe it, Sergeant. I could tell you about supreme court justices, senators . . ." He coughed, wiped at his mouth with thin dry hands. "Point is, I met Marilyn. I was having a drink with a friend, and there was this dancer. It was like one of those films in which an older upstanding man falls for a beautiful but disreputable girl. A gap in age as well as social class. But I fell, Sergeant. And hard."

Kelso said, "Yes, sir," and gave him just the hint of an encouraging smile.

"She liked me, she seemed to fall for me. We developed a kind of relationship. She needed extra money, and I gave it to her. I saw her once a week, on Thursday evenings, and gave my wife the excuse that Thursdays would always be devoted to after-hours work—depositions, meetings in chambers, and so forth. In other words, I fed her some legal talk and big words, and she bought it. She respected my mind and my work."

Kelso thought, How unfortunate for her, and said, "I see."

"I suppose my secretary told you that part of it. I've reason to believe she did."

"Well, we spoke to her . . ." He shrugged.

"Exactly. Well, Sergeant, I've reason to believe that Marilyn Strauss shot my wife to death Tuesday night."

The judge sat back in his wooden chair and fell silent, his lips tight and grim under the bristle of his mustache, his bushy eyebrows bunched over his dark eyes and hawk nose. He'd spoken his piece. It was Kelso's move.

Kelso took a yellow notepad from his desk drawer, clicked the top of a ballpoint, and assumed a businesslike attitude.

"Can you tell me why you believe this, your honor?"

"Certainly. She spoke of it from time to time."

"What?" Kelso looked up sharply, no longer acting a role.

"I said, she spoke of it. Starting approximately two weeks ago, she began telling me how she wished something would happen to Barbara, and several days ago she said she'd give anything if somehow Barbara could be made to die."

"I thought you only saw Marilyn on Thursdays."

"That's true. But we spoke often over the phone. And the last time I saw her, last Thursday, the seventh, she said it in person. She told me she couldn't stand it any longer, that she had to have me for herself, she couldn't keep sharing me. She said if I refused to divorce Barbara, then Barbara would probably have a fatal accident."

"Why on earth didn't you tell somebody about this?" Kelso asked irritably. "You knew there was a threat against your wife, and you just let it go?"

The judge nodded grimly. "I understand how it sounds to you, but at the time, Sergeant, I didn't take it the least bit seriously. Remember, Marilyn Strauss is a nightclub dancer, she's a hard tough girl, used to lying at the drop of a hat. It was just the kind of thing she'd say simply to shock me, jar me into some kind of decision. I took it as bluff, not a genuine threat. She didn't strike me as a murderess."

"But now you believe it was a genuine threat."

"Definitely."

"Simply because it happened?"

Boller shook his head. "No. I'm a judge. I demand more than mere speculation. But there's such a thing, you know, as circumstantial evidence." He paused and narrowed his eyes even more. "Have you gotten the autopsy report yet, Sergeant?"

"No. It's expected soon. Why?"

"It'd be interesting to know what weapon was used."

"Really?"

"Yes. Last Thursday night in her apartment, Marilyn showed me something she'd picked up for herself. It was a revolver."

"What make and caliber?" Kelso asked immediately.

"I only glanced at it. She didn't say—probably didn't even know—but I'd guess it was a .38. The point is, five days prior to the murder of my wife by means of a gunshot in the head, my mistress, who'd already indirectly threatened to kill her, showed me a revolver."

Kelso made more notes on the yellow pad and asked: "All right, Judge Boller, is there anything else?"

Boller stood up. "No. I've used enough of your time, and I've got a meeting." He glanced at his watch, as if to emphasize it. "I just thought you should be made aware of all this."

Kelso stood, too. The judge was an inch or so taller.

Kelso looked up at him and said: "Thanks. I appreciate it." He wondered if the judge could hear the irony in his tone.

"Not at all." Without offering to shake hands, Boller turned and strode quickly from the duty room, leaving Kelso scowling at the door. After a minute or two he bent over his desk and read what he had written on the pad:

Boller slept around instead of with wife—fell hard for Marilyn—thinks Marilyn wanted his wife dead—Marilyn got a .38 revolver?

The door opened and Smith came in, holding a sheaf of papers which he brought over and tossed down on his desk. "Well," he said angrily, "we're in a hell of a fix now."

"Really? Don't tell me the canteen's out of Danish?"

"It's worse than that. This is the goddamned autopsy report."

"Oh yes?"

"Yes. And guess what?"

"They found a dog's paw prints on the woman's throat," Kelso guessed.

"Dr. Paul was right," Smith said. "Mrs. Boller was shot with a .38 revolver from an estimated distance of two to three inches." He sat down, lit a Kent, and crossed his feet on the desk, puffing smoke and scowling at Kelso.

"Well," Kelso said. He, too, sat down, feeling suddenly tired. "Then we're back at square one. Footprints in the snow."

"What'd the judge want?"

"Oh, he was very amusing. Now he claims that his wife's been frigid for some time, which forced him to sleep with young topless dancers. Says he fell in love with Marilyn Strauss, who recently bought herself a revolver, possibly a .38, and talked about getting rid of Barbara Boller."

"Was he putting you on?"

Kelso shook his head glumly. "No, I don't think so."

"What's he mean, *possibly* a .38? Did he get a look at it?"

"She showed it to him, but apparently they don't teach firearms identification in judge school."

"Ah." Smith nodded. "Well, what'd you get from the computer?"

"Nothing yet." As if by magic, his phone rang. He picked it up. "Kelso here."

"Hi, George. This is Cindy, in the computer room."

"Yes? What'd you get?"

"What you asked me for. You can come down and pick it up. But basically it's negative, except for one thing."

"Can you tell me," he asked, "or do I have to guess?"

Chuckling, she replied: "There's no record of anybody named Roy Welsh. As for Marilyn Strauss, she doesn't have a police record, but something interesting happened to her about ten years ago."

"What happened?"

"She was the prosecuting witness in a rape case, and guess who the presiding judge was?"

Kelso didn't have to guess. "Henry Boller," he said.

Smith was eyeing him curiously.

"Yeah," Cindy Raintree said. "How'd you know that?"

"I'm a detective. Listen, I'll be right down. Okay?"

"Sure thing. You want to have lunch? Or coffee?"

"Some other time."

"I'll give you a rain check."

"Thanks." He hung up and looked at Smith. "Get this. Ten years ago, Marilyn Strauss was the prosecutrix in a rape case tried by Boller."

Smith looked interested. "Hmm. Which means Boller's lying if he says he's only known her a short time. That's interesting, but I don't exactly see any connection between that and his wife's murder."

"I've got a feeling there's a connection," Kelso told him. "I think we need to ask Marilyn Strauss a few more questions. Suppose she cried rape and they tried the case and let the guy off, and she's been furious ever since?"

"Then," Smith said, "she'd want to kill Boller, not his wife."

"Exactly. And that's what happened. Somebody tried to kill Boller. That wasn't his wife the killer saw in the yard, or thought she saw. She went there to kill *him,* and she thought she did."

"Then what's this bullshit Boller just gave you about Marilyn threatening to kill his wife?"

"I don't know." Kelso got up and zipped up his parka.

Smith shrugged. "I don't like it. It doesn't fit together very neatly. Boller acquits some creep Marilyn claimed raped her, then she waits ten whole years before doing something about it? And not only that, but after ten years, she sleeps with him before trying to kill him? I don't like it."

"Let's go talk to Marilyn," Kelso said. "Maybe the pieces will start falling together after a while."

"This is nuts," Smith said.

They stopped off at the computer room on their way out. Cindy Raintree had the computer analysis ready in a beige folder, which she handed to Kelso with a big smile.

"Here it is, George. Now, about lunch—"

"Thanks," he said hurriedly. "But I'm sorry, I already told you, Smith and I are on our way out. We're investigating the Boller case, and there's a big push on it."

"Don't kid me, George. I know very well you eat no matter what. Doesn't he, Karl?"

Smith nodded. "Yeah, it's unusual for Kelso to miss a meal. I remember once, though, when there was a tornado, he skipped breakfast until the all-clear sounded—"

"Let's go," Kelso said, giving Smith a look.

Smith grinned. "Tell you what, Cindy, how about my buying you lunch? I'm not in as much of a hurry as Kelso."

"I have to eat with my girlfriend," Cindy Raintree said politely. "But thanks for asking me, Karl. Maybe tomorrow, okay?"

"Yeah. Sure."

In the lobby, Smith buttoned up his heavy coat and said: "I don't get it. She's always coming on to you, Kelso, but she won't give me the time of day. What's she see in you that she doesn't see in me?"

"You're probably too tall for her. After all, she's only about five-two. Tall men sometimes intimidate short women. And, other than that, it's probably just that I radiate a certain aura, a combination of vibrant personality and erotic—"

"Shove it, Kelso."

"Right."

They went out into the snow, where the clouds had been replaced by a high blue sky with lots of glaring sunshine and frigid temperatures, so that their shoes squeaked on the frozen pavement. They got into Smith's LTD and drove to 523 South Central Avenue and when they parked at the curb it was 10 A.M.

They got out and went up to the door.

Twenty-four

It was a huge old brick building with an expansive lobby and numbered mailboxes. It wasn't a security building; cheap rent doesn't include safety. They went down a hall and rode a rickety elevator up to three, then turned left and knocked at the door of 3B. A white card tacked to the wood above a brass knocker had M. STRAUSS printed on it in blue ballpoint.

There was no answer. They knocked again. It was chilly in the hall, but brightly lit.

"Maybe she's out baring her tits again," Smith muttered, and pounded so hard on the door with one of his giant fists that Kelso thought he would break it down. Instead there was a click and the door came loose and opened slowly inward.

"She must be nuts not to lock her apartment," Kelso said.

"She did lock it," Smith observed. "The lock's been forced."

Kelso saw splintered wood. Smith's knock hadn't done that, but a crowbar or similar tool had.

Instantly, they were on the alert. Kelso unzipped his parka and put his right hand on the handle of his holstered .38. Smith, whose sheepskin coat was already unbuttoned, reached inside for his shoulder holster.

"I'll cover," Smith said.

"Okay."

Smith drew out his .357 and aimed it toward the door. There was no one visible in the hall. Kelso drew his .38, cocked it, and counted out loud: "One . . . two . . . three . . ." As he said the word "three," Smith kicked the door hard with his right foot, sending it banging inward.

Kelso charged into the room, crouched low, holding his revolver extended in both hands and glancing left and right.

Smith followed him.

The living room was empty of people. It was cheaply but comfortably furnished, and you could tell a woman had done it—the colors were light, there were a couple of prints on the wall, there were flowers in three different vases. Kelso could see dust rising in the beam of sunlight filtering in through frilly yellow curtains. At the far right, a door stood partly ajar.

Kelso advanced, weapon still ready. He and Smith stood at either side of the door, counted three silently, and stepped through into a small kitchen with a few unwashed dishes in the sink and part of a cup of coffee on a counter.

"Other door," Smith said.

In the living room again, they looked at a closed door opposite the one to the kitchen. The procedure was the same as when entering the apartment. A count of three, Smith kicked the door open, Kelso entered, Smith followed.

It was the bedroom, yellow shade pulled over the window, bed neatly made and covered with a comforter with a bright flowery design in green and yellow, closet door open to reveal clothing on hangers, bathroom door open and nobody in it or in the shower.

They walked around to the other side of the bed and stared down at the floor between the bed and the window.

Marilyn Strauss lay there, on her back, arms out to the sides, legs slightly parted. She wore a green V-necked sweater over a light green shirt, dark green wool skirt that had ridden up to her mid-thighs, beige hose, green flats. There was what looked like a gunshot exit wound in her forehead, just over her left eye, and on the gold wall-to-wall carpeting blood had formed a large blotch under and around her short black hair.

They checked the entire apartment again, quickly, and then outside in the hall, but there was nothing else.

Then they returned to the bedroom and stood looking down at her body while Kelso called headquarters on his portable radio and Smith holstered his revolver and crossed his long arms over his chest and muttered: "Jesus Christ."

Twenty-five

When the crime unit got there and went over the dead girl's apartment, nothing of any particular interest or use was uncovered. There was no firearm of any kind, no ammunition, nothing to indicate that Marilyn Strauss had recently owned or possessed a weapon of any sort. They found a kind of diary, but its contents were mundane—memos to pick up bread and milk at the corner grocery, get clothes back from the cleaners, that sort of thing.

There was a list of telephone numbers in the back of the diary, and one of them was Judge Henry Boller's residence. If she had called him at his office, she'd looked up the number or, in any case, felt no need to write it down. The other numbers proved to be a cleaners, two movie theaters, a pizza place, the B & P, and her mother in Portland, Oregon.

None of her dancing costumes were in the apartment; apparently she had kept those in the nightclub dressing room.

Dr. Paul arrived and examined the body, then came into the living room, where Kelso sat reading over the computer results he'd received from Cindy Raintree.

"Looks like close range with a medium-to-large-caliber bullet," Paul said. "I'd guess it was a .38. Bullet blew out a lot of brain tissue and left the usual exit hole. She's been dead about four hours, maybe a little longer, but of course that's approximate."

"Of course." Kelso frowned. "Five or six this morning? Well, it'll be interesting to know if it was the same gun that killed Barbara Boller."

"Yes, it will. Do you have a gun yet, in the Boller case?"

"No. Not yet."

"Well, if you don't need me, I've got some work to do."

"Take it easy," Kelso said.

Smith came in from the hall as the doctor left. "As usual," Smith said, "nobody heard or saw anything this morning while a woman was being noisily shot to death with an elephant gun. I wonder if they'd have noticed a wrecking ball knocking down the goddamned building?"

"Probably not," Kelso said. "Did you ask them about the early morning hours? According to Dr. Paul, it was probably between five and six—"

"Hell, yes, do you think I'm some rank amateur? I *have* been a detective for a while, you know. What's that you're reading? A comic book?"

"Report on Marilyn Strauss. I was looking at the part about her rape trial. It's kind of interesting."

"Why?"

"Because there wasn't an acquittal after all. The guy charged with raping her was convicted and got ten years."

"I just thought of something," Smith said. "How old is Marilyn Strauss now?"

"According to her driver's license, twenty-five."

Smith nodded. "So, ten years ago, when she was raped, she was only fifteen. In other words, a minor."

Kelso closed the folder and got up from his armchair. "Yes?"

"It's just that I happen to know a little about the rape laws. If you rape a minor, consent isn't an issue. It becomes immaterial, or irrelevant, or whatever the lawyers say."

"In other words, it might not've been forcible rape."

"Yes. Exactly." Smith looked glum. "Not that it helps us at all. It's just a point of interest."

"Well, you're right. About the law, I mean. According

to the information Cindy got from the court records, he was charged with having had sexual intercourse with a minor. His defense was that he'd never been anywhere near her, but the prosecution was able to convince the jury that he was lying."

"Does it say that?" Smith asked. "That the jury didn't believe him?"

"No, but he was convicted."

"Well," Smith said, starting to button up his sheepskin coat, "that gets us exactly nowhere. Ten years ago Marilyn Strauss has sex with some idiot who's convicted of statutory rape. Then she becomes a topless dancer and falls in love with Judge Boller, and threatens to murder his wife. And, sure enough, his wife is murdered. Shortly afterward, the judge comes to you, wringing his hands and confessing his sins about having cheated on his wife with this slut. And shortly after that we find her shot dead in her apartment."

"And," Kelso reminded him, zipping up his parka, "there were no footprints in the snow."

"Other than those of Judge Boller and his dead wife and their stupid little dog."

Kelso sighed. "You're right. It really doesn't get us anywhere at all."

A uniformed patrolman named Krause came out of the kitchen with one of the crime-scene investigators, a plain-clothes fingerprint expert named Hubbard. Smith, about to leave the apartment, turned to Hubbard and said:

"Listen, Eddie, let me know if you find any dog prints around here, okay?"

Hubbard stared. "Huh? *Dog* prints?"

"Yeah. You know—the paw prints of a little dog?"

Smith sauntered out into the hall. Kelso started after him, and Hubbard said:

"Dog prints! Sometimes I think Karl Smith's just plain out of his mind." He shook his head.

"It's possible," Kelso told him, "that both murders were committed by a small black poodle wearing a red knit sweater." He gazed at Hubbard for a moment with a perfectly straight face, then turned and went out into the hall.

Before leaving the lobby, he and Smith checked all the other mailboxes, but none bore the number 217. They got inside Smith's LTD and drove off in the cold bright sunshine.

Twenty-six

Meyer stood in the computer room and ogled Cindy Raintree. He felt that he was what a police detective should be—well dressed, businesslike, sharp-witted, inquisitive, able to see through the varicty of bullshit dished out by the average civilian. Last week he'd gone out with a girl quite a bit younger than his own thirty-six and a half. She had recently purchased the soundtrack LP from some weird movie called *Repo Man*. Her favorite song on the album was "Pablo Picasso," and she had played it for Meyer. A line from the song had stuck in Meyer's mind and now was going round and round. Something about being only five feet three and never called an asshole.

I'm much taller than five foot three, Meyer told himself. I'm five foot seven. Almost. And girls can't resist my stare. And nobody ever calls *me* an asshole.

Cindy Raintree was perhaps four inches shorter than Meyer, which made him feel even taller. She looked Jewish, with red hair and dark eyes, a slightly dark complexion (tanning booth, Meyer thought), a rather sharp little nose, very busty. It was the glint in her dark eyes and the smirk on her very pretty lips and her bustiness that especially attracted Meyer. She *is* busty, he thought. She does have nice tits. If you play your cards right, he told himself, you could talk this little girl right into bed.

"Raintree," he said, trying a smile. "Is that your married name?"

"I'm not married, Sergeant. You know that."

"Oh yeah. I forgot. Listen, about that number I asked you to search—"

"You're lucky," she told him. "A lot of towns in the state wouldn't have been able to help you with it. But Clairmont City's got a data base for street numbers, filed with the county assessor, and a program for querying it without writing a new program. You understand?"

Meyer had no idea what she was talking about, and didn't particularly care, as long as he got what he wanted. "Sure," he said.

"You must be very smart."

"That's what they say."

"So I checked it for you, and found fifteen street addresses in the city with the number 217."

Meyer scowled. "Fifteen? Jesus, I was hoping for one or two."

"I was expecting about twenty-five or thirty. Fifteen's not so bad. You can check out fifteen addresses, can't you, Sergeant?"

She beamed at him and Meyer smiled back briefly. She was wearing a green sweater and a wool skirt, and that sweater was really filled out. He looked up at her eyes; she was smirking again.

"Anything else I can do for you, Sergeant?"

"Huh? Well, give me the addresses." She handed him a sheet of paper, which he folded and pocketed. He'd read it later. "Say, it's getting close to noon. What're you doing for lunch?"

"Me?"

"Sure. As it happens I don't have much on for the next hour or so, and I've got to eat, right? So why don't me and you find a nice quiet place and I'll buy you lunch. Whatta you like? French? Italian? Greek?"

"I hate Greek."

"How about French? We could—"

"Sergeant Meyer, I'm sorry, I'm busy for lunch."

"Oh yeah." Meyer gritted his teeth. Was she playing hard-to-get, or didn't he appeal to her? It was his shortness, he was certain of it. Or the fact that he was Jewish—which, now that he thought about it, she probably wasn't. Raintree. More like an Indian of some kind. So he was too short and too Jewish. He glared at her.

"Maybe some other time," she told him, smiling politely. "Okay?"

"Sure. Well, goodbye." He turned to go.

"Have you seen George around, Sergeant?"

Meyer stopped and looked back, glaring. "George who?"

"Sergeant Kelso."

"I'm not his goddamned baby-sitter," he said, and stalked out.

In the detective section, Meyer found Broom at his desk, leafing through a large volume of some kind.

"What's that you're reading?" Meyer asked.

"Trial transcript."

"Huh. Is it related to the Boller case?"

Broom smiled. "Yes, it is."

Meyer sighed and bent over his own desk. Broom was always smiling, he reflected. He didn't understand people who smiled all the time, especially men. It wasn't natural for a grown man to be that happy. He wondered if Broom had a screw loose. He unfolded the report Cindy Raintree had given him.

It consisted of fifteen city addresses with the number 217. Meyer sat down, lit a cigarette, and scowled at the list:

217 Arnold Avenue
217 Dirk Drive
217 East St. Clair Street
217 Edison Street
217 Fillmore Lane
217 First Street
217 Hedley Street
217 Magnus Drive
217 Main Street
217 Nineteenth Street
217 O'Toole Street
217 Palmer Avenue
217 Phillips Road
217 South Central Way
217 Third Street

Meyer thought for a while, puffing at his cigarette, then picked up his phone and dialed the exchange number for the computer room.

"Data Processing," a husky voice said.

"Raintree?"

"Yes?"

"Detective Sergeant Meyer. Listen, about that list you just gave me, why aren't there any apartment numbers on it? There must be a hell of a lot of apartments numbered 217."

"The county assessor's data base is for taxable property only," she explained. "For rental property, only the buildings themselves would be listed, not individual apartments, since apartment renters don't pay property tax."

"So can you search for apartment numbers?"

He thought he detected a sigh before she answered:

"No, Sergeant, there's no data base for apartment numbers. Not in this city."

Meyer scowled. "Goddamned computers," he said. There was no reply. He visualized the girl's bust, rising and falling with her breath. "Say, how about reconsidering on lunch?"

"I'm sorry."

"How about dinner tonight?"

"I've got to go now, Sergeant. Someone's here."

"Give me a break, Raintree."

"Goodbye, Sergeant." She hung up.

Meyer slammed down the receiver. When he looked across the room, Broom was smiling serenely at his trial transcript. Meyer stood up.

"Broom! Come on, we've got to go out."

"Oh?"

"We've got fifteen addresses to check out, and see if one of 'em fits this key."

"Certainly." Broom got up, looking pleased, and put on his coat. He was young and plump and altogether too damned pleasant. Meyer scribbled a quick note to himself about data bases, decided he didn't know what it meant and threw it in the trash, then went out into the hall with Broom.

"Are you doing anything for lunch, Broom?"

"Not that I know of."

"Wanta grab a bite with me?"

"I'd be glad to."

"Okay." Sighing, Meyer buttoned his coat. Broom wasn't so bad. They'd go to a restaurant and maybe he'd meet a nice waitress. Fifteen addresses, he thought.

The key was in his coat pocket.

Twenty-seven

Kelso and Smith reached Judge Boller's office at two minutes after eleven. In the outer office, Mrs. Noonan glanced up through her bifocals, nodded curtly, and said:

"I'm sorry, he's in court." Glancing at the tiny silver watch on her thick wrist, she added: "I expect him back before eleven-thirty." This morning she seemed rather subdued.

Kelso nodded. "Thanks. We'll wait, if you don't mind."

"Suit yourselves." She went back to her typing, and for a time there was only the clatter of the keys, the dry hiss of Kelso's pipe, and the occasional slap of Smith's shoes on the tiled floor as he paced from one end of the small room to the other, looking annoyed.

Kelso sat down in a wooden chair and tapped out his pipe. He longed for a cigarette; he hated the tobacco companies for having manufactured products that were so addictive and at the same time, at least according to the government's reports, so harmful. All he wanted was a little pleasure in life. Existence is a garden of flowers, he thought, but they all had bees hiding in them, waiting to sting.

He thought about the judge. He would be in court now, while the guilt or innocence of various humans was decided. Of what was the judge innocent, and of what was he guilty?

Had he found some diabolical way of trudging out into the new-fallen snow without leaving his tracks, to murder his wife? And had he then decided that his mistress,

Marilyn Strauss, knew too much? And had he, therefore, shot her as well?

No gun was registered to Boller, but that meant nothing. Many citizens, as Kelso well knew, considered it a God-given right to possess firearms and saw nothing wrong with failing to register them with the police. They bought them out of state, or in sleezy back-street shops, or from friends and relatives and even vague acquaintances. They didn't bother with permits and laws.

He frowned. It had looked so clear at one point: it had seemed that Marilyn had shot Mrs. Boller. But now she was in the morgue and it wasn't so clear. Boller could have acquired a .38 revolver and carried out both shootings, easily.

And then there was that key.

"Good morning, gentlemen."

Kelso glanced up. Boller had just stepped into the office from the hall, still in his robes. His frown was tight and formal. Smith stopped pacing.

"Morning, your honor," Kelso said. "Could we see you for a minute or two? Something's come up."

The judge's black eyes darted from Smith to Kelso a couple of times; then he shrugged, nodded, touched a finger to his mustache, and said: "In my chambers."

They followed him, and remained standing while he went around the desk, set down a heavy volume, removed his robe and hung it on a rack, then took his chair and rocked back slightly, gazing at them. Kelso thought he could detect a slight twitch beneath the judge's left eye.

"So, what's so urgent?"

"It's Marilyn Strauss," Kelso said quietly. "She's dead."

He and Smith watched. The judge rocked a couple of times, the chair squeaking. He frowned hard. The twitch became more obvious. He shook his head.

"How'd she die?"

"She was shot," Smith said. "Somebody blew her brains all over her bedroom floor, with a .38, probably. Close range. Just like your wife."

The judge's black eyes closed and opened slowly. Like a reptile, Kelso thought.

"I see. And do you know who did it?"

"Where were you between five and six this morning?" Smith asked.

"What difference does it make?"

"Just answer the question," Smith snapped.

"I'm not obliged to answer any questions. I'm not—"

"Did you kill her?"

"Don't be absurd."

"Would you mind telling us where you were?" Kelso asked.

Boller glared. "I mind very much. But if it'll get you out of my office, I'll tell you. I was in bed, asleep. My alarm went off at a quarter till seven, as usual. Period. Anything else?"

"In other words," Smith said, "you can't prove where you were between 5 and 6 A.M."

"That's exactly right."

"When's the last time you saw Marilyn Strauss?"

"Alive?" the judge asked, with a hint of irony.

"Either way," Smith said.

Boller shrugged. "I don't recall. Last week, I suppose. Thursday."

"Your usual night out, in other words," Smith said.

Kelso saw Boller's face close up like a locked safe.

"You have any other questions, gentlemen?"

"Let's suppose, your honor," Kelso tried, "that you didn't shoot Marilyn Strauss. That seems a safe bet to me. Let's suppose she was merely a good friend of yours. Do you have any idea who might've wanted her dead?"

"Sergeant, I told you I had no idea who'd want to kill my wife, and for Marilyn Strauss the answer doesn't change. I don't have any idea. Now, if you'll excuse me . . ."

"Do you remember a trial about ten years ago?" Smith asked. "Involving Marilyn Strauss?"

"I've never . . . I don't recall that Marilyn Strauss was ever charged in my court."

"That's not what I mean. She wasn't charged. She accused. She claimed she was raped, and the rape trial was in your court. Statutory rape, as a matter of fact. Marilyn was fifteen. You remember?"

Boller stared. Kelso could find no expression in the man's eyes, but a muscle in his jaw twitched. Boller touched his mustache again and said gruffly:

"I only vaguely recall it. I've tried a number of rape cases over the years. Is there some point?"

"Was the guy convicted?" Smith asked.

"I haven't the slightest idea."

"Didn't you sentence him?"

"I don't recall."

"Maybe he was acquitted. Was Marilyn very upset about it at the time?"

"You're wasting your time, Detective Smith. And mine. I suggest you obtain a copy of the trial transcript, if you've got questions about it. I'm not a walking courtroom encyclopedia." He stood up.

"Your honor," Kelso asked politely, "were you in Marilyn's apartment very often?"

Judge Boller frowned. "I was . . . there on occasion."

"I just wondered. You see, the place was fingerprinted, and we're having all the prints checked out. So, in case we find yours there, I just wanted to get the record straight."

"That won't help you, of course."

"We just have to check everything," Kelso said. "By the way, you did tell me that you saw a revolver in her apartment?"

Boller scowled. "Yes."

"Interesting," Kelso said. "There wasn't one in there when we found her body."

"Good luck with your investigation," Boller said.

They moved to the door. Smith paused on the way out to add:

"Incidentally, Judge, the guy *was* tried in your courtroom, and he was found guilty of raping Marilyn Strauss."

Boller shrugged and looked grim.

* * *

In the hall, Smith asked: "Well, Kelso, what do you think?"

"About what?"

"Did he kill her?"

"I don't know. He's acting awfully strange, but I'm not sure what it means. Besides, it doesn't make sense. If he killed his wife so he and Marilyn could be together, then why kill Marilyn? And if somebody else killed his wife, he'd have even less motive for getting rid of Marilyn. Either way, it doesn't make sense."

"There's one way it makes sense," Smith said. "Marilyn killed Mrs. Boller. Then Boller, who still loved his wife even while sleeping with Marilyn, killed her as revenge."

"Sounds like a soap opera," Kelso said.

"Well, he acts guilty about something."

"He probably is."

"Is what?"

"Guilty about something," Kelso said. "Are we eating lunch now?"

"I suppose."

They passed the green benches and the lawyers, rode down to the third floor, and entered the duty room. Meyer and Broom were out. McNutt was at his desk, scribbling on a notepad and munching a sandwich. It felt cold. Leill's door was shut.

There were no messages. Not that Kelso had expected any. I'm missing something, he thought. But he couldn't decide what it was. Sighing, he went out again, with Smith. Maybe it would come to him.

Twenty-eight

Meyer and Broom split up, Meyer taking eight of the addresses and Broom the other seven. Meyer had thought carefully about this. If he'd insisted on taking only seven, Broom could have decided that Meyer was being unfair. By allowing Broom to take the lesser number, Meyer came off as the good guy.

"I'm letting you have it easy," he told Broom, just in case it hadn't occurred to the plump detective. "I'm giving you one less address, since there's an odd number."

"I'd be glad to take the extra one myself," Broom said, smiling cheerfully.

"*I'll* do it," Meyer insisted. He tried to sound weary, but it came out as anger. "I've got more experience, and I'm older. I'll do it. Meet me back at the office when you've finished."

First they had gone to a small restaurant two blocks from the Municipal Building, but he hadn't gotten lucky; their waitress turned out to be a guy. Afterward they parted, and Meyer drove off in his blue unmarked cruiser toward the first address, 217 Arnold Avenue.

He was not in a good mood. The traffic had turned the streets to slush, which was constantly thrown up onto his windshield, forcing him to use the wipers and washer often. Driving always made Meyer nervous; he was easily intimidated, and felt that people were always trying to run over him. Sometimes he longed to be back in uniform just so he could arrest a bunch of these clowns.

The Arnold Avenue address was in a near-downtown

area of small houses, shops, bars, and older apartment buildings. Number 217 was a tiny brick house set virtually on the street with no place to park. Meyer stopped in front, by a fire hydrant, got out, rang the bell, and waited. It was cold; he shivered in his overcoat, and the harsh wind ruffled his thin black hair. His mother would've insisted that he wear a hat, but he didn't have to worry about that now. Hats are stupid, he thought, and the door opened.

A tall thin black girl looked out at him, about twenty-five, not bad-looking, wearing a blue sweater, faded jeans, and brown loafers. She had nice hair and a good complexion about the color of coffee with cream.

"Yes?" Her voice was soft, pleasant.

"Detective Sergeant Meyer. City police." He held up his I.D. folder.

The girl's eyes flitted to the badge and photo card, then met Meyer's gaze again, steadily, innocently, without fear. She even smiled a little.

"What can I do for you, Detective Sergeant?"

He wondered if he was being mocked. She was taller than he was, forcing him to look up at her. He hated it.

"What's your name, miss?"

"Alice Glenn." She spelled it.

"You live here alone, Miss Glenn?"

"I live here with my husband, Edward Glenn. Would you mind telling me what this is about, Detective Sergeant?"

"It's about this," Meyer said gruffly. "I've got a key I think may belong to you. I'd like to try it on your door and see if it fits."

"Just like Cinderella," the woman said, smiling. She had very white teeth.

"What the hell's that mean?"

"Nothing at all. Don't you remember the glass slipper?"

"I don't know about glass slippers, lady," he snapped, and took out the plastic bag. It was useless. The key wouldn't even go all the way into the lock. He tried several times and quit.

"You ever see this key before?"

"No, I haven't."

"Could I see your front door key?"

"Certainly." She stepped back into the house, then reappeared with a brown leather handbag. Rummaging inside, she brought out a ring of keys and gave it to him with one separated from the others. "That's the front door key," she said.

"All right." Meyer tried it; it easily fit and worked the lock. He scowled at the other keys, then held each against his, but none matched. He gave up. "Here," he said, shoving the key ring back at her.

"I'm sorry I couldn't help you, Detective Sergeant."

"Yeah. Look, have you had this lock changed lately?"

"No, it's been on the door slnce we moved here, over a year ago." Somewhere in the house a baby began crying loudly. "I'm sorry, I have to go now. Was there anything else?"

"No. Goodbye."

"Goodbye, Detective Sergeant." Smiling, she closed the door.

Meyer, feeling like a complete idiot, trudged back to his cruiser, got in, and sped off for the next address.

"Bastard shoots a broad dead and leaves his key," he muttered. "Probably found it in a gutter and it's nobody's key. Wild-goose chase." He sounded his horn at a woman trying to back her Pinto into the street without looking.

Meyer drove to seven more addresses with the number 217 and repeated the procedure, with minor variations. The result was totally negative. His key fit none of the doors in question and did not vaguely resemble any keys shown him by any of the residents. It was a washout. Furious, he returned to headquarters and stomped into the detective section to find Broom sitting serenely at his desk, apparently engaged in gazing out the windows at the downtown buildings.

"What the hell's going on?" Meyer asked. "Are you finished already?"

"Certainly." Broom turned to smile at Meyer. "But I've only been back about five minutes. Did you have any luck?"

Smiling simp, Meyer thought. "No, I didn't have any luck. What about you?"

"None at all." Broom looked quite happy.

"That's just great," Meyer snapped, trying to irritate the fat young idiot. "Just damned great."

"It was probably to be expected," Broom said. "You know, it's pretty unusual to find a house key with the street number stamped on it."

"Huh?"

"Most keys with numbers are for apartments, or hotel and motel rooms, sometimes for storage lockers."

Meyer sat down and hunched over his desk without answering. The fool was probably right. Which meant, he thought bitterly, that they were in worse trouble than ever. According to Cindy Raintree, there was no way to run a computer search on apartments and hotels, and there were probably a lot more than fifteen of them with the number 217. It might take hours, or days, maybe even weeks, to locate and check them all.

He took the plastic bag from his coat pocket, dumped the key out onto his desk blotter, and glared at it while he lit a cigarette. "Damned key," he muttered. And then, just in case Broom hadn't heard: "Goddamned key!"

The key lay there on his blotter, glinting dully in the glare from the overhead lights, the number 217 mocking him. He scowled at it for a long time, then shook his head, crushed out his cigarette, and returned the key to its plastic bag.

Twenty-nine

Kelso and Smith ate lunch at a cafeteria four blocks from the police parking lot. There was Muzak and lots of Early American decor, and a huge fireplace with a real fire. Kelso had country-fried steak and Smith had his usual vegetable plate. They ate without talking. Then Smith said, lighting a Kent:

"Let's go up to the Boller place again."

"I agree," Kelso said. "I want a better look at that yard."

"Any theories yet?"

"Not really, but I keep thinking about the alley behind the house, and Agnes Street. Both of them were cleared of snow."

"Yeah?"

"Someone could've approached along either the street or the alley without leaving tracks. What if the killer came down the alley and crawled over the fence and into that evergreen tree?"

"And then what?" Smith asked. "He still had to get close to the back of Mrs. Boller's head with a revolver."

Kelso sighed. "It's impossible."

"I thought of something. What if Boller's wife got much closer to that tree than we think, almost touching it, for example? So that someone hiding in it or behind it only had to poke the gun out through the branches?"

"But she wasn't lying that close to the tree."

"I saw a man shot in the head once, Kelso. In the Army. I won't bore you with the gory details, but here's an interesting thing: the bullet entered the back of his head, just like with the judge's wife, and he went down. But he managed to crawl about three yards, turning his head from side to side, before he collapsed and died."

"Hmm. So you think Mrs. Boller . . ."

"Could've been shot near the tree, then crawled to where she was found."

"It's a possibility," Kelso admitted. "But there are two things I don't like about it. One, there were no indications in the snow that she'd crawled. Between her body and the tree, the snow was fresh. And two, it makes it into a pure accident, pure chance. The killer couldn't have planned for her to get that close to the tree. You said yourself that the whole thing looks planned, calculated, including the fresh snow on the ground. The killer had to be able to kill Mrs. Boller while she stood a couple of feet away from the tree."

Smith glared and leaned back in his chair. "He could've planned to shoot her from under the tree, right in her face, or in her chest. She'd have been just as dead. Maybe the plan was to fire from the tree, no matter what."

"In any case, we've got to face the facts. And the facts are that she stood a few feet from the tree and, nevertheless, was shot in the back of her head at close range, by somebody who didn't leave footprints in the snow." He lit his pipe, then added: "And don't forget. There's still the problem of the key."

"Yeah." Smith slid out of the booth. "The damned key."

In Smith's LTD, they drove north, out of the downtown sector. It was 1 P.M., traffic was heavy, and the sky was a brilliant blue.

Kelso leaned back in his seat, feeling depressed. The investigation was not proceeding by leaps and bounds.

Smith blew his horn at a pedestrian who was crossing in the middle of the street. It was a young blonde holding a baby in one arm. With her free hand, she gave Smith the finger.

"Is it me?" Smith asked. "Or has society just literally gone down the drain?"

"It's society," Kelso replied. He looked at the young mother. He wondered what her baby would grow up to be like.

Eventually they arrived at Wadding Way and the intersection with Agnes Street. On their left was the judge's house. Smith turned into Agnes, then into the alley, and parked. They got out and stood gazing at the scene.

Everything looked different in the daylight. They faced south, squinting into the early afternoon sun at Boller's house. Kelso walked up to the white wooden fence that enclosed the yard, and stood looking at the tall evergreen in the corner of the lot. Dozens of tracks still remained in the snow, left by Mrs. Boller, her dog, and all the police investigators.

Smith put on his tinted aviator sunglasses and joined Kelso at the fence.

"I think there are more tracks than before," Kelso said.

"Birds and animals," Smith told him. "Look out your window some night after midnight, and just see all the creatures that come nosing around, looking for food. It's amazing."

"I'm interested in human animals right now," Kelso said, moving along the fence closer to the tree. He was trying to imagine that he had come here to commit a murder, with a revolver, with a fresh layer of snow on the yard. Ten P.M.—time for Henry Boller to walk his dog, a poodle that would head straight for the evergreen tree.

The tree was tall and pyramidal, like the traditional Christmas tree, very wide at the base. The bottom branches touched the snow. By leaning forward and resting his gloved hands on the top railing of the fence, he was able to put his face practically into the branches.

"What're you doing?" Smith asked suspiciously.

"Getting ready to commit a murder," Kelso said.

He climbed over the fence and put his feet down in the judge's yard, between the fence and the tree. Branches poked him. Crouching low, he crawled under the tree. Now he was completely hidden from outside view; at least, he thought so.

"I think it's possible," he called to Smith.

"Good for you." Smith's voice came from nearby. "You get a merit badge."

"Do me a favor."

"I don't lend money to friends."

"Go around to the front of the house, then come across the yard, toward me. Pretend you're walking a dog."

"Do you want me to be the judge or his wife?"

"What difference does it make?"

"I'm a method actor," Smith said. "I have to know about the character I'm playing."

"Give me a break, Smith."

"Okay, okay. Hey, Kelso, do you want me to pretend that the dog is pissing in the snow?"

"If it makes you happy."

"I'm already overjoyed."

"Hurry up. These needles are scratching me."

"Where's Kelso?" Smith said, moving away from the tree. "Why, he's under the tree, pretending to be a killer." He muttered something Kelso didn't catch, and his voice faded.

The wind sighed in the branches. A cardinal flew into the tree and then, startled by Kelso's presence, made a noise and flew away again. Kelso waited, sitting on his haunches, growing cold. He was able to peer out through the greenery and see Boller's house.

Presently Smith appeared, walking along the side of the house, actually holding out one hand as though he had a dog on a leash. He seemed to be saying something; as he approached, moving in a curious zigzag fashion rather than a straight line, Kelso could make out the words:

"Attaboy, attaboy. No, don't go that way, we don't want to go that way. Here's your favorite tree, boy. See your tree? It's your favorite place to make wee-wee. Attaboy. Don't pull so hard on the leash, or I'll tie you to a passing truck. Are you warm enough in your darling little sweater that granny knitted just for you? Here's your tree. Now you make wee-wee while I stand here and see if anybody materializes behind me with a loaded pistol. If I get shot, run to the house and telephone the police, okay?"

Kelso thought Smith was very funny. Sighing, he waited for him to get within a couple of feet of the tree, then pointed his right index finger, cocked back his thumb, and slowly eased his hand through the branches and out into the open. He aimed his index finger at Smith, who stood approximately where Barbara Boller had, just before she'd fallen.

"Can you see my hand?" Kelso called out.

"Of course I can," Smith replied. "But it's broad daylight. What'd you expect?"

"It might've been different at night."

"What are you aiming at?"

Kelso sighted along his finger. "Your chest. Or your head. Depending."

"Not the back of my head, then?"

"Definitely not the back of your head. You'd better fall forward into the snow."

"I'm not falling into the goddamn snow," Smith said.

"In that case," Kelso said, "the play's over." He sighed, pushed his way out from under the tree and into the yard, and straightened up.

"So much for your little production number," Smith told him.

"There's no way I could've gotten my hand even two or three feet from your head," Kelso said glumly. "Much less two or three inches. And how'd I get the key onto your back?"

"It was all done with mirrors," Smith replied. "Let's go. My feet are getting wet and I'm probably going to catch cold, and it'll all be your fault."

"I hate this." Kelso was depressed. He'd had the notion

that if they could just reenact the crime, things would somehow fit together. Instead it all seemed that much more impossible.

"I keep telling you, Kelso, the dog did it. How'd you like my walking-the-dog act, by the way?"

"Leave your name and address and we'll get back to you."

They went over the fence, got inside the LTD, and left.

At two o'clock they were back downtown. In the detective section the duty room was empty but smelled of stale tobacco smoke.

"Wouldn't it be funny," Kelso said, "if somebody high up decided to get rid of Boller and hired a killer to shoot Barbara Boller and then Marilyn Strauss, just to set Boller up?"

"It'd be hilarious," Smith said. "And also stupid. They didn't leave enough evidence to frame Boller. Besides, why not just kill him?"

A folded piece of notepaper lay on Kelso's desk. He picked it up, unfolded it, and read:

> Kelso: I have gone out of town for three days. The upstairs pressure I spoke of has intensified. I expect you to make an arrest before my return. I trust you comprehend the importance of this in relation to your future with the Department.—R. Leill, Lieutenant, Detective Section.

"I don't believe it," Kelso said, handing the note to Smith. "Is he for real?"

Smith read the note, then chuckled. "Jesus, Kelso, we work for one weird asshole. You want this back?" Kelso shook his head. Smith wadded up the paper and tossed it into his trash can. "Well, now that your job's on the line, I guess you'd better find somebody to arrest."

"Let's forget about the judge for a while," Kelso told

him, "and concentrate on Marilyn Strauss. The B & P's open at this time of day, isn't it?"

"Sure."

"Let's poke around over there, see if we can find somebody who knew Marilyn personally, talk to the bartenders and waitresses and whatnot. Okay?"

Smith shrugged. "We don't have much else to do."

"Maybe you'll be able to make a date with one of the dancers."

"I don't date sluts."

Just then Broom came into the duty room, smiling cheerfully.

"Hello," he said. "I've just been doing some research into that rape trial. It's very interesting."

"What'd you find out?" Kelso asked.

"Some things that tie Judge Boller and Marilyn Strauss and the rapist all together in one package," Broom said.

Thirty

Kelso and Smith had been about to leave again. Now they went to their desks and sat down. Smith lit a Kent and Kelso got out his pipe but didn't light it. Broom strolled over to his desk by the windows, sat down heavily, smiled, and said:

"The defendant was a person named Donald Clark, and his case was unusual. For a rape case. He was caught in the act."

Kelso raised his eyebrows. "In bed, you mean?"

"Yes. The police entered his bedroom at eleven one evening and found him in bed with Marilyn Strauss, who had just turned sixteen years old. There were several strange things about it. It was never really explained how the police happened to go to Clark's apartment just when he was in bed with the girl."

"Interesting," Smith said.

"Clark's defense was that he never actually, uh, joined with the girl."

"Are you talking about penetration?" Smith asked irritably.

Broom smiled at him. "Yes. Penetration."

"It's not exactly a dirty word," Smith said.

"Yes. Well, that was his defense. But the rape law at the time provided that penetration could be proved by the . . ." Broom opened a notebook and peered at it. "By the uncorroborated testimony of the prosecutrix."

"What's that mean?" Smith asked.

"It means," Broom explained, "that if the only testimony was the girl's, saying he penetrated her, and the defendant denied it, the jury could simply decide to believe the girl without any other proof."

They all sat thinking about that for a minute.

"Hell of a law," Smith said.

"It's supposed to protect rape victims," Kelso said.

Broom nodded. "Exactly, George. Anyway, that's what happened. Marilyn Strauss testified that she and Donald Clark had made love. And here's another interesting thing. Clark waived his right to counsel and defended himself."

"Damned fool," Smith muttered.

"Why'd he do that?" Kelso asked.

"It turns out that Clark had some legal training. Two years of law school before flunking out. Now, get this: fourteen years ago, his criminal law professor was Henry Boller."

Kelso stared. Smith started to chuckle and lit another Kent.

"So they knew each other," Kelso said. "That's amazing."

"It was just before Boller's appointment to the bench. He'd been an assistant prosecutor for a while, then on the staff of the state attorney general. He taught law for two years, and was made a criminal judge. That's not in the trial transcript, of course. I found it from some news items." Broom beamed proudly. "One last thing—Clark called one witness besides himself, a girl named Sheila Terman." Broom looked very smug.

Smith said: "He wants us to ask him who she is, Kelso."

"Well," Kelso said, "I suppose we'd better, then. Broom, who is Sheila Terman?"

Stanley Broom nodded. "She was Marilyn Strauss's best friend. By the time of the rape trial, they were both out of high school and sharing an apartment together. Donaid Clark tried to get Sheila to testify that he'd never had, uh, sexual relations with Marilyn, but her testimony wasn't allowed because she had no direct way of knowing about it."

Kelso gazed at the plump, smiling Broom. "You wouldn't happen to know the current whereabouts of this Sheila Terman, would you?"

"I haven't found her address yet, but I did some asking around, and it turns out she's working as a waitress at—"

"The B & P," Smith finished for him.

"That's right, Karl. How'd you know that?"

"It fits," Smith said. "Too damn well."

"It's only logical," Kelso said, zipping up his parka again. "Maybe it was that blonde you were ogling last night."

Smith got up. "Let's go find out. Broom, that's really excellent. You want to come along with us to the club?"

"No, thanks. I'd better write up my report."

Broom was a stickler for reports.

Smith shrugged. "Okay. Well, come on, Kelso. Let's go check it out."

Kelso felt mildly excited. He was trying to assimilate the new factors, correlate them, see if they fit together into a nice new picture of the case. He thought they did, but he wasn't exactly sure how. His mind raced, and he felt slightly edgy, as if he'd had too much coffee.

He thought it would be very interesting if it turned out that Marilyn Strauss and Sheila Terman had shared an apartment numbered 217.

They drove to the B & P and Smith parked his LTD on the street. It was two-thirty on the afternoon of Thursday, January 14, cold and clear.

The place was nothing like it had been the night before. The stage was empty, the music was from a jukebox turned down low, and a soft dim glow, rather than strobing lights, pervaded the room. It felt very warm. Kelso unzipped his parka.

Only a few customers sat at tables or the bar. Behind the

counter a white-shirted bartender was speaking to a young blond waitress.

"Is that the one from last night?" Kelso asked.

"I think so, but I'm not certain."

He glanced at Smith. "You're not certain? That's one for the books."

They took a table near the wall, folded their overcoats on the chairbacks, and after a moment the blonde came over. She set down two glasses of water and two napkins and smiled vaguely. It was the one from the night before. In the surer light, Kelso saw that she was heavily made up, with red lipstick and black eyeliner. Her daytime costume consisted of a black sleeveless blouse, black leotards, a short black skirt, and black flats.

"Help you?" she asked, opening her order pad.

"Seven-Up," Kelso said. "How are you?"

"I've been better." She glanced uncertainly at Smith. "And for you?"

"Black coffee," he said.

She scribbled on the pad. "One 7-Up. One coffee, black."

"We were in here last night," Smith said. "Remember?"

The vague look left the blonde's eyes. "Oh yeah. The guy in love with the stripper."

"Say," Smith said, "you wouldn't happen to know Sheila Terman, would you?"

She gave him a strange look. "Yeah. I know her. But obviously *you* don't."

"What makes you say that?" Kelso asked.

"Because I'm Sheila Terman, and I don't know you guys from Adam."

"We'd like to ask you a couple of questions," Kelso said.

"Yeah? What about?" Then she frowned. "Hey, are you guys cops?"

"It's about Marilyn Strauss," Smith said.

Kelso saw something in her eyes, a kind of flicker. She seemed on the brink of walking away, but suddenly her scowl softened, and she pulled over a chair, sat down, and said:

"Okay. Ask."

"We understand," Kelso said, "that you and Marilyn were friends back in high school."

Sheila stared at him. "How the hell'd you know that?"

"Do you remember that Marilyn was seeing a guy at the time, a law professor named Boller?"

"Give me a break, okay? Marilyn never dated any professor. What kind of crap is that?"

"Are you sure?" Kelso asked politely. "We were told she did."

"She dated a law student," Sheila said. "Not a professor."

"A law student." Smith nodded. He got out a Kent and lit it. Kelso could feel the tension. He thought they might be on the verge of something.

"Who was this student?" Kelso asked.

"I don't remember."

"Sure you do," Smith told her cheerfully. "It was Dan something or other, right? Or, maybe not Dan. Maybe Ron. Wait, I know—it was Don. Right? Donald."

"It could've been."

"Sure it was. Good old Donald. Hey, Kelso, you remember Donald?"

"Donald Clark," Kelso said softly. "Right, Sheila?"

She blinked. He was trying to read her face; there might have been fear there, but he wasn't sure.

"Are you afraid of us?" Smith asked.

"Of you guys? Don't be silly."

"What *are* you afraid of, then?"

"Not a damn thing."

"I've got to use the facilities." Smith got up and headed toward the back. It was something they did occasionally with reluctant witnesses. Smith made them nervous, and Kelso was pleasant. Then Smith would go away for a while and Kelso would try to get them to confide in him. Sometimes it worked.

"Sheila," he said, "we're investigating the murder of Marilyn Strauss. Did you know she was killed?"

The waitress's black-lined eyes were dull.

"Of course I knew it."

"This is tough for you, I suppose. But we're only doing a job."

"Yeah. Well." She shrugged.

Kelso thought that fifteen years ago she'd been a teenager, probably cute or pretty and still full of ideals. Slightly fifteen years before that, she'd been a pink fat baby in someone's crib, fresh home from the hospital, the innocent victim of something called birth and parents. Theoretically she'd had an equal chance, along with all other babies, of growing up to become a happy and successful adult. But only theoretically. In reality, she was already doomed—by virtue of her family, or her housing project, or her genetic makeup, or countless other negative factors—and would have very little chance.

A scientist with all the facts, Kelso reflected, might have been able to look at baby Sheila and observe that she would grow into a sullen, cynical, tough waitress in a topless bar, involved in rape and murder.

He wondered what would be done with such a baby when that kind of prediction could be made with high reliability.

She was watching him, hostile and suspicious. He felt the usual frustration at wanting to make some kind of human contact with her but knowing the impossibility of it. He was well aware of the wall between them.

He could only do his job.

"Did you and Marilyn stay pretty close, after all these years?" he asked.

"Yeah, I suppose. More or less." She shrugged again. "I don't stay too close to anybody. It doesn't pay. You know?"

"Yes. I know."

"You just get burned, if you get too close."

"Yes," he said. "It's too bad."

"Do you know who shot Marilyn?" she asked.

Kelso shook his head sadly. "Not yet. We've got a few leads. We're just trying to figure out what her situation was, who she knew, what she was doing . . ."

"She wasn't doing drugs, if that's what you think."

"No. I didn't think that."

"So what's all this stuff about Donald Clark?"

"We're trying to find out if there's any connection between the two of them."

Sheila Terman stared hard at him for a moment, then asked:

"Are you kidding? You really don't know?"

"Know what?"

"Shit, what a riot." She glanced around toward the bar, where the white-shirted guy was carrying refills out to a couple of working types. "Look, I've gotta get back on duty. Donald was a law student that Marilyn dated a few times. He was weird, you know? I mean, he liked young girls. See?"

"Sure."

"Like, he was already pushing twenty-five, and me and Marilyn were just sixteen. That's how he got into trouble."

"Are you talking about the rape case?"

"Yeah. The rape case. See, he got set up by somebody. I don't know who. He had Marilyn over at his place one night when the cops busted in and arrested him for doing it with a minor. I think it was just before her sixteenth birthday." She chuckled. "What a laugh. When Marilyn was fifteen, she could've passed for twenty-one."

"Did Donald know how old she was?"

"Sure. He wasn't stupid. He was *glad* she was under-age, that's how he liked 'em. He tried putting the make on me once or twice, but I turned him down. I wasn't sharing anybody with my best friend."

"I see." So, he thought, at sixteen Sheila Terman still had something resembling a code of ethics.

"Anyway, the moron wouldn't hire a lawyer, because he'd been to law school for a while. And look what it got him. Ten years in the pen. As a matter of fact . . ." The dull look returned to her eyes. "Forget it."

"As a matter of fact, what?"

"Nothing. It doesn't matter."

"So," Kelso said, "Donald Clark went to prison, you and Marilyn became roommates, and neither of you dated Henry Boller?"

"Isn't that the judge who sent Donald to prison?"

Kelso said nothing. At the far end of the bar, Smith emerged from the back and caught Kelso's eye. Kelso frowned and shook his head very slightly. Smith nodded and rested against the bar.

Sheila glanced quickly around the room again, then leaned closer to Kelso. "I think it's the other way around, if you really want to know. Look, Marilyn wasn't dumb, she knew Boller framed Donald on that rape charge. But she was sorta naïve, you know? Boller started hanging around in here, several months ago, and buying her drinks and stuff."

"Judge Boller bought drinks for Marilyn?"

"That's what I said. And then they'd go up to her place, and she told me they were making it. Right?"

"Yes," Kelso said, nodding.

"So I asked her, 'What the hell are you doing, making it with a bastard like that, old enough to be your father?' And she said she just had a kind of thing for him. And then his wife got shot, I suppose you guys know about that?"

"We're looking into it," Kelso replied blandly.

"I expect you are. Well, can't you imagine that Marilyn was scared to death after that? I figure it this way. Boller thinks Marilyn shot his wife. So he comes after her and shoots her, to get even. Whatta you think?"

Kelso couldn't tell if he was being kidded or not. "To tell you the truth," he said, "we've considered that possibility."

"I think Boller killed Marilyn," Sheila said.

"Who do you think killed his wife?"

She shrugged. "How should I know? Well, I have to go."

"What about Donald Clark?" Kelso asked quickly. "Marilyn didn't still have any feelings for him, did she?"

"No. He was just a guy she dated once or twice. But, there's one other thing you oughta know about Donald, in case you don't already."

Smith stared hard from the end of the bar counter, but Kelso shook his head again. "I'd like to know," he told the waitress.

She lowered her voice more. "When Donald was in law school, he took a course from Boller, and he said he was going to ace it. We asked him how, since he couldn't even make C's in most anything else. And he said he had Boller in his pocket."

"In his pocket?"

"Right. So I asked him how. And he said he was letting Boller use his apartment, you know, Donald's place, to shack up with various girls. Like Marilyn, for instance. See, the bastard was married and he was cheating on his wife."

"Let me get this straight," Kelso said. "This was back before the rape trial, when Donald Clark was in law school, and Boller was teaching law?"

"Right."

"Clark was in one of Boller's classes, and was letting Boller use his apartment to cheat on his wife?"

"You got it. And Clark aced Boller's course. He really did."

"That's very interesting."

"You still don't get it, do you?" Sheila narrowed her black-lined eyes. "See, when Donald got busted for sleeping with Marilyn, he called up Judge Boller and reminded him of how he used to use his apartment. He tried to talk Boller into letting him off with probation, but Boller sent him up for ten years." She gave a low laugh. "Donald didn't ace *that* course."

"Do you mind if I ask how you know all this?" Kelso asked.

"Marilyn told me. It's what Donald told her."

"Let me ask you one last question, Sheila. Did you ever talk to Marilyn about what happened on the night Donald Clark was arrested?"

"Yeah. Once or twice."

"Were they actually, uh . . ."

"You're an awful prude for a cop. Yeah, they were."

"Did Marilyn say there was penetration?"

"Penetration? You mean, did he screw her? Of course he did." She got up. "You want anything with that 7-Up?"

"No thank you."

"You can tell your friend he can come on back now." Smirking, she went back across the wooden floor to the counter.

Smith strode over to Kelso's table and sat down.

"Well? It took you long enough, Kelso. What'd she do, tell you her life story?"

"I think we're onto something."

"Really?"

"When Donald Clark was in law school, he was letting one of his married professors use his apartment to sleep with girls. In return, the professor gave Clark an A in the course."

"Don't tell me," Smith said. "The professor was Boller."

"You get an A-plus."

"I was always bright in school."

"Something else," Kelso said. "Apparently Marilyn Strauss and Donald Clark actually did have intercourse the night he was arrested."

"Huh. How would our waitress know that?"

"Marilyn told her."

"Of course, the waitress could be lying. Or Marilyn could've lied to her."

"I don't think so."

Smith smirked. "She must've gone for you, Kelso. Did you make a date with her?"

"Of course not." He frowned. "Anyway, the other

thing is, when Clark wound up in Boller's court on the rape charge, he tried to talk him into suspending the sentence, apparently reminding him of their previous arrangement. But this time it was no go, and Boller gave him ten years."

"Which means," Smith said, "that Clark had a darn good motive for killing Boller."

"Sheila Terman could have a motive, too. She denies being very interested in Clark, but suppose she was? Suppose she hated Boller for sending him to jail, and hated Marilyn for sleeping with Clark. She might've shot them both."

"It'd be nice to have some real proof for a change," Smith said. "Instead of this endless speculation."

The blonde brought their drinks. "You guys want anything else?"

"Where were you Tuesday night around ten o'clock?" Smith asked, a little abruptly.

"Here. Working. You can ask Eddie, the guy behind the bar."

"What about this morning between five and six?"

"I was home. In bed."

"Oh yeah? Can you prove that?"

"I was in bed with Eddie," she said. "You can ask him."

Smith looked disgusted. "Never mind."

"Thanks, Sheila," Kelso said, smiling. "We appreciate it."

"Come again." She smiled back, glared at Smith, and hurried away.

The jukebox played again. The two working guys finished their beers and left. An old man ordered another tall something. At the bar, a guy in a plaid hat ordered a sandwich.

"Let's go," Smith said, standing up. Then: "Hold it a minute." He went over to the counter and said something to the bartender, who glared and said something loudly.

Smith took out his I.D. and said something that sounded like: ". . . better believe it!"

The bartender muttered something, scowled in Kelso's direction, and shrugged. Looking smug, Smith headed for the exit and Kelso followed.

Outside, Kelso asked: "What was that all about?"

"Interrogation. He confirms the blond broad's alibi. She worked here Tuesday night, and he spent last night with her at her place."

"I forgot to get her address," Kelso said suddenly. "I've got to go back."

"No you don't. I do my job, after all. Eddie the bartender gave me both addresses, his and hers. You want to guess whether either of 'em is 217 anything?"

"I don't want to guess," Kelso said.

"The answer is neither."

"Aren't we lucky."

They got into Smith's LTD and drove away. Clouds were starting to move in from the west, dimming the afternoon sun. Something that had been said recently, or left unsaid, was gnawing at Kelso's mind, as though an insect had tunneled into his brain and was trying to find its way out.

Thirty-one

When they entered the detective section duty room at nearly three-thirty, Detective Sergeant Meyer scowled up from his desk like a small dark bird. Smith waved cheerfully and said:

"Hello, Meyer. How was your day? Justify your paycheck?"

"Just be quiet and listen up, you guys. I've been working my tail off, as usual."

"I think you should be put in for a bonus," Smith told him, sitting down at his desk and putting his feet up.

"Yeah. Well, anyway, I got on the phone and started calling up apartments. You guys ever look in the Clairmont City yellow pages and see how many apartments are listed?"

"A lot?" Smith asked.

"Three or four," Kelso said, removing his parka and sitting down.

"Screw both you guys. I didn't count 'em, but there's a hell of a lot. And I called every one of 'em and asked if they had a number 217."

Kelso had to admire the little detective's industriousness. He himself would never have wanted to tackle that job, though he'd known it might be a good thing to try.

"What'd you come up with?" he asked.

"I came up with nineteen apartments with a number 217."

"That's not very many."

"No, it's not. But there's a reason. Lots of places number their units with floor numbers and letters, so it's 3A and 6B, and so on. Also, some of 'em are big complexes, like yours, Kelso, where the numbers are actually street addresses.''

''Well,'' Smith said, no longer grinning, ''you've got a list of nineteen apartment buildings with the magic number. So now what? Do we take the key around, the way you and Broom did with the houses?''

''Broom and I'll do it,'' Meyer said. ''So what've you and Kelso come up with? Anything?''

Kelso told him.

Meyer said: ''You should talk to whoever prosecuted the rape case, and also those arresting officers. We should have a record of all that.''

Broom, who had been sitting quietly at his desk, now spoke up: ''It's in the trial transcript. The officers were two uniformed patrolmen named Allen Arkowitz and Richard Hunt.''

''So where the hell are they now?'' Meyer asked.

''I thought of that,'' Broom said mildly. ''I checked with personnel. Arkowitz moved out of state one year after the case, at just about the time Donald Clark's appeal was denied. And Hunt was shot in the line of duty three weeks after that, while attempting to resist an armed robber.''

''So where's Arkowitz now?''

Broom shrugged his rounded shoulders. ''Personnel doesn't know. He seems to have disappeared. His last known address was a box number in Phoenix, Arizona, but his mail is returned from there marked 'No Forwarding Address.' ''

Kelso thought about the power wielded by high-up politicians, even criminal court judges. He thought about Henry Boller's arranging for someone to shoot Patrolman Hunt in the ''line of duty,'' and arranging for Patrolman Arkowitz to quit the force and disappear somewhere in Arizona.

''That's very convenient for certain people,'' he said.

Smith chuckled. ''This case is beginning to smell.''

Meyer glared. ''What about the prosecutor on the case, Broom? Don't tell me something happened to him, too?''

"No," Broom replied. "Nothing happened to him. His name is Edward Sterns."

Kelso and Smith exchanged glances, and Smith's white eyebrows went up high.

"Edward Sterns," Smith said, "is chief deputy prosecutor for felony trials. Probably going to run for prosecuting attorney next year."

"I hear he and Judge Boller play a lot of golf together," Kelso said.

Meyer shrugged. "Well, somebody's going to have to talk to him. See if he knows anything about all this."

"Smith and I'll talk to him," Kelso said.

Broom and Meyer left to visit the apartments on the list, and Kelso and Smith went down to the second floor, where the county prosecutor's offices were, and sat on straight-backed wooden chairs in a reception area, waiting to see Sterns.

On one of the other chairs sat a thirtyish woman in a long coat, sobbing softly from time to time, her face bruised around both eyes and one side of her mouth. A battered wife, Kelso thought glumly.

Some crimes were almost beyond his comprehension.

After a few minutes, a door opened and Sterns appeared in shirt sleeves, his tie loosened at his unbuttoned collar. He looked impatient.

"Come in, gentlemen," he said. "I can give you about five minutes."

They went in. Sterns stood behind a large metal desk and peered solemnly at them through gold-rimmed glasses. The office was rather tidy, books neatly arranged on shelves, papers neatly stacked on top of the desk, suit coat and overcoat hung neatly on a corner rack.

"What can I do for you, gentlemen?"

Kelso and Smith were standing, since they hadn't been offered chairs and, in any event, were in a hurry.

"I'll get right to the point," Smith said. "Ten years ago, you prosecuted *State versus Clark*. A guy named

Donald Clark was charged with statutory rape on a sixteen-year-old girl named Marilyn Strauss. Henry Boller tried the case. Do you recall it?''

Sterns lit a cigarette with a chrome-plated lighter, snapped the lid shut, puffed smoke, and said:

''How would I remember a rape case from ten years ago? Was it some kind of landmark thing? I don't remember any Clark case.'' He spoke in a rather high nasal whine. Kelso had heard that whine in court; after a time, it could get on one's nerves.

''It was a little unusual,'' Kelso said. ''Clark was caught in the act, so to speak. Two patrolmen entered his apartment one night, around eleven, and found them together in bed. And Clark defended himself, since he'd had some legal education.''

''Sorry.'' Sterns shook his head. The expression on his face was perfectly blank. ''Don't remember it. Look, I'm in a rush. I've got a woman out there whose husband beat her up, and I've got a preliminary hearing, and a suppression hearing, and some arraignments—''

''I suppose you've got some kind of record of the cases you've tried,'' Smith said. ''I mean, you *do* keep records, don't you?''

''What's all this about, anyway?'' Sterns asked. ''I mean, is it important?''

''How important is the Boller murder case?'' Smith asked.

''Judge Boller's wife?'' Sterns blinked twice. He puffed at his cigarette. ''How's that related to a ten-year-old rape case?''

''That's what we're attempting to find out,'' Smith said. ''Without much cooperation from the people we talk to about it.''

''You don't have to get snide,'' Sterns said. ''My office cooperates with the police in all cases. We have a very good relationship with the police.''

''Great,'' Smith told him. ''Then you can look up the Clark case and see about it.''

"Just exactly what am I supposed to be looking for?"

"We'd like to know why two uniformed patrolmen entered a girl's apartment at eleven o'clock at night."

"Isn't there a trial transcript?"

"We looked at it," Kelso said. "The patrolmen had been given an anonymous tip, and their informant's name was withheld."

"Quite proper and customary, gentlemen."

"So you don't remember anything else about it?" Smith asked.

"Gentlemen, there really are so many rape cases. They come and go. Donald Clark? I'll check my records, but I'm not going to be able to provide you with much more than you've already got in the transcript. I promise you."

"Let us know if you find anything unusual," Smith said.

Sterns glanced at his watch. "Of course. Now, if you'll excuse me, gentlemen . . ."

Kelso and Smith left. In the reception area the battered wife was sobbing again. She got up and went past them into Sterns's office, and they could hear him talking to her in his shrill nasal voice. He'll make her feel a lot better, Kelso thought.

"You think he'll give us anything?" Smith asked, as they climbed the stairs to the third floor.

"As a matter of fact," Kelso said, panting slightly, "I think he's been bought off."

"I think you're right. We may be up against a political wall here. Judge Boller may have shut the door on us."

The duty room was deserted. It was going on 4 P.M. Outside the windows, Kelso could see snow falling again.

"What do you think would happen if we followed Boller for a while?"

Smith frowned. "If you want my honest opinion, I think we'd drive around town and watch him eat his dinner somewhere, and then we'd follow him to his house, and we'd freeze our asses sitting in front of his house, and at ten o'clock he'd walk his stupid dog, and then we'd go home and go to bed.''

''That's a possibility,'' Kelso admitted.

''Or, we could forget the whole thing, eat supper, then go over to my place for a drink and a game of chess. You owe me a rematch, you know.'' He paused. ''Unless you and Susan . . .''

''Supper and chess sounds fine,'' Kelso told him. ''But I really think we should take a chance on following Boller tonight. It's Thursday.''

''Kelso, the broad he was playing around with on Thursday nights is in the morgue with a bullet hole in her head.''

''Maybe he had more than one girl lined up. Maybe he'll go visit Sheila Terman.''

''I'll go with you,'' Smith said. ''But if nothing happens, you owe me a dinner and a game of chess.''

''Deal.''

They put on their coats, checked their revolvers, and went out.

Thirty-two

The telephone at the B & P rang, and Eddie the bartender answered it. Sheila Terman was waiting on customers in one of the booths. It was 4:15 P.M., and the supper business was starting to pick up. In forty-five minutes the strobe lights would be turned on and the live band would start playing; an hour later the dancers would come out.

Sheila smiled at the two guys in the booth, a couple of young prosecuting attorneys in blue three-piece suits, white shirts, and ties. Strange, she thought, that such men came to a place like this. But they left good tips, so she smiled and bent low so they could see plenty of cleavage.

When she took their orders to the counter, Eddie said:

"Hey, Sheila. Phone call for you. Take it in back, and don't talk too long, okay? It's getting busy."

"Thanks, Eddie."

She went to the back room marked PRIVATE and picked up the phone. "Yeah?"

"It's me," a gruff voice said.

She recognized Judge Boller's voice immediately.

"What the hell do *you* want?"

"It's about Marilyn," he said. "The police may ask you about her."

She gripped the receiver tightly, thought how much she hated him, and said nothing.

"You mustn't tell them anything, Sheila."

"Oh yeah?"

"It's in everyone's best interest." The judge's voice was hard. She could hear his breath, raspy and quick.

"Why's it in my best interest? I didn't kill anybody. I don't have anything to hide."

"The police might decide you killed Marilyn." Boller paused. His raspy breathing grew louder. "They might even decide you killed my wife."

In spite of her anger, she felt afraid. Her hand sweated on the telephone receiver. You murdered your goddamned wife, she thought at him. And you murdered my best friend. But she drew in a deep breath and said quietly:

"I already talked to the cops. I didn't tell 'em anything."

"I'd prefer that they not know about my connection with Donald Clark."

Her pulse quickened. She lied. "I didn't mention his name."

"Good. Please don't. Do you understand? Do not mention him in regard to me. I hope that's clear."

"Perfectly."

"Goodbye, Sheila."

She heard the dial tone, then replaced the receiver and stood for a minute or two, trying to get her breath and make her heartbeat return to normal. After a while, she gritted her teeth and went out of the private office, along the hall, and back into the bar.

"Who was it?" Eddie asked.

"My mother," she said, and carried drinks over to the young smirking prosecutors.

Thirty-three

"There he goes," Kelso said.

He and Smith were in his VW, after an argument that Smith had lost, parked in a no-parking zone across from the Municipal Building. It was 4:30 P.M., Thursday, the fourteenth of January, and a light snow was falling from a darkening sky. The streetlights were coming on. It was drab and cold and depressing.

The huge metal door to the underground parking lot, reserved for high-up officials, had opened, and Judge Boller's yellow Cadillac was nosing up the slanting ramp to the street.

"That's a particularly revolting shade of yellow for a Caddy," Smith announced.

"If you want a yellow car," Kelso said, "a Volkswagen's the best way to go."

"I hate Volkswagens."

The argument had been because Smith detested small cars, especially Kelso's, which never seemed to be working quite properly and, in addition, took a long time to heat up in very cold weather. There was greater warmth and much more leg room in Smith's LTD; on the other hand, it looked too official, with its big spotlight and radio antenna. So Smith had reluctantly agreed to go in the VW, which by no stretch of the imagination could have anything to do with the police.

"Go now, go now," Smith urged. "Can't you see you're losing him?"

"I'm not losing him," Kelso said, pulling the VW into

traffic and accelerating to keep up with Boller's car. "I'm just hanging back a little."

"There's no reason to stay back in this traffic, Kelso. He won't be looking for a Beetle, and if you get too far behind, you'll lose him at a red light."

"I won't lose him," Kelso said.

They drove in silence for a few minutes. Boller drove north on Central Avenue.

"Obviously," Smith said after a while, "he's not going to any nightclub. He's headed directly home."

"I wonder if he knows how to cook," Kelso murmured.

"Can't we have some heat now?"

"It's on. It just takes a while."

"I can't stand it."

The Cadillac continued north. Gradually the business district fell behind and Central Avenue became a wide residential street bounded by large yards, tall trees, and expensive homes.

"This reminds me of Meridian Street in Indy," Smith said, lighting a Kent and rolling down his window an inch. "Ever been there?"

"Of course I have." It was dark now. Oncoming headlights glared into Kelso's eyes, but he kept Boller in view. The traffic flow was uniform, and Boller was cruising at a constant thirty-eight miles an hour, the normal rush-hour rate in this thirty-five-miles-per-hour zone.

"Do you like it?"

"Not particularly. Clairmont City's about as big as I can take."

"There are only a hundred thousand people in this city," Smith said. "It's more like a large town."

"I don't mind large towns," Kelso replied. "But cities depress me. Indianapolis. Chicago. Louisville. They all depress me."

"He's turning, Kelso."

"I can see that."

Boller turned northeast on to Sherwood Avenue and Kelso went through the intersection on the yellow light.

"He's going home," Smith said testily. "Just like I told you he would. But you never listen to me."

"Maybe he knows somebody who lives in this neighborhood."

"Maybe they'll invent a drug that prevents crime."

When the judge turned onto Wadding Way several minutes later, Kelso was forced to admit that it was probably a lost cause. Boller pulled into his driveway and braked. The automatic garage door slid up, the garish yellow Cadillac eased forward into the garage, the door shut. The garage lights went on, then off. The lights in the house came on, first one room and then another, until the entire first floor was lit. The drapes and curtains remained closed.

They sat in the VW, opposite Boller's house, the engine running.

"We can't just sit here all night," Smith remarked.

"Let's wait for a while and see if he goes out again."

Smith sighed.

An hour later, nothing had happened.

"I give up," Kelso said.

"About time."

He had been running the engine twenty minutes on and twenty off, something he'd read somewhere to do but couldn't recall the reason for. It was off now; he started it, made a U-turn, and headed downtown.

"Dinner and chess?" Smith said. "According to our agreement . . ."

"Dinner and chess," Kelso muttered. Suddenly the insect in the back of his head ate through into his consciousness. "Oh my God, I just thought of something we didn't check."

"Can't it wait?"

"Donald Clark. He let Boller use his apartment, to take girls there."

"Yeah, yeah. We've been over all that, Kelso."

"Boller took women to Clark's apartment," Kelso said. "Clark let him use it. How do you suppose they set it up?

Clark wouldn't have been there when they arrived. He'd have given Boller—"

"A key!"

"Yes," Kelso said. He felt excited for the first time since the start of the investigation. "The key."

Thirty-four

Cindy Raintree had left for the day by the time Kelso and Smith got back to the Municipal Building. In the duty room, Meyer and Broom had also gone. McNutt was just leaving and had no idea where anyone else was. No one had left a note. Leill, of course, was still out of town—very conveniently.

"This is one hell of a way to run a detective section," Smith observed, sighing and lighting a cigarette.

"What we need is the transcript of that trial," Kelso said. "Broom was reading it." He went over to Broom's desk and tried the drawers, but they were locked. Shrugging, he went to gaze out the windows. Outside, it was dark; the store lights, traffic signals, and auto headlamps glistened on the wet streets. "On the other hand, maybe we don't need the transcript."

"What are you talking about, Kelso?"

"Donald Clark's address would've been listed in the transcript, and if it'd been 217, Broom would have told us. So Clark wasn't living at 217 anything at the time of the trial."

"Maybe before the trial, though," Smith said. "Maybe when he was letting Boller bring sluts to his apartment."

Kelso nodded. He was beginning to think that Clark was the key to the case. If Clark had lived at a 217 address at the time of Marilyn's rape, and the key fit that door, and it was the one Boller had used . . .

"Let's go get something to eat," he said.

* * *

They had a late supper at Hunter's and sat looking out the large plate-glass windows at the steadily falling snow that already was sticking to sidewalks and curbs. The ceiling lights glared on the Formica-topped tables, and over the clatter of dinnerware they could hear faint music: Percy Faith's "Theme from *A Summer Place*." Kelso ate meat loaf, green peas, and mashed potatoes, followed by peach cobbler for dessert; Smith had a plate of peas, creamed carrots, and Brussels sprouts, with raisin cake.

"Suppose," Kelso said, "Donald Clark decided to kill the judge for sending him to prison for a rape he may or may not have committed, despite the fact that Clark had loaned the judge his apartment key for a while, so the judge could cheat on his wife."

"Okay," Smith said. "I'll suppose that."

"Suppose Clark got out of jail, watched Boller's house, and noticed that every night at ten o'clock Boller walked his poodle."

"That's what he'd have noticed, all right."

"He got himself a .38 and hid by that spruce tree, because he also noticed that the poodle always went there. And somebody came out and led the dog to the tree, but Clark didn't realize it was Boller's wife."

"So he fired anyway, and Mrs. Boller dropped dead in the snow."

Kelso nodded. "And also suppose Donald Clark's got a kind of absurd sense. You know—a sense of irony. He thought it'd be appropriate to leave his old apartment key on the judge's body. So he tossed it down."

"Tossed it down?"

"That's another thing. The absence of footprints in the snow is a problem. But he could've tossed the key right out from the tree. As a kind of spiteful final gesture."

"Huh," Smith said. "But you still can't explain why he didn't leave any footprints."

"I'm only supposing," Kelso said.

"Well, what about Marilyn Strauss? Who killed her?"

"Maybe Clark killed her, too. She must've known

whether he actually had intercourse with her that night. Maybe she lied on the stand."

"Two cops went in and found them in bed."

"Maybe," Kelso said, "the cops lied, too."

"You're implying that Boller somehow bought off all those people—two patrolmen, a sixteen-year-old girl, and possibly her friend Sheila. What would be the point?"

"You mean, why would Boller want Clark convicted of rape? I've got a theory, but I don't know . . ."

"Tell me the theory, Kelso."

"What about this? Boller was up for an appointment to the criminal bench. He had a good record, a good name. No skeletons in his closet, not that anyone knew about. Then along came Clark and reminded him of the apartment and the girls Boller took there, while married, and maybe Clark threatened to tell someone about it."

"In other words, blackmail."

"Exactly. So picture yourself as Boller. With no scruples. And some idiot's trying to get money from you, and you're about to become a judge. What would you do?"

"Hire a hit man."

"Be serious."

Smith shrugged and lit a cigarette. "You want me to say I'd arrange to have Clark charged with rape. I'd talk some teenaged girl into testifying against him. I'd have a couple of cops bust into the guy's apartment on a night when I knew the girl would be there."

"Exactly," Kelso said. "And then who'd believe him? A convicted child rapist. He could make all the accusations he liked, all about keys and apartments, and Boller would simply shrug and say, 'Well, convicted rapists will say anything.' "

"That's a pretty cynical outlook, Kelso. Congratulations."

"Thanks." Kelso drank down the last of his coffee. "Let's go to your place. I want to make a couple of calls."

"There's a phone here, by the rest rooms."

"Yours is nicer, and your coffee's free."

* * *

At his apartment, Smith made a pot of coffee and set up the chess board while Kelso used the living room phone.

"Broom? This is Kelso."

"Hello, George."

"When you were reading about the Clark case, did you happen to notice how long Boller had been on the bench prior to Clark's arrest?"

Some people might have had trouble answering that question, but Broom had an eye and a memory for details, along with the knack of deciding which details were important.

"Yes," Broom said in his pleasant voice, "I did notice. In fact, Boller was appointed to the bench ten days after Clark's arrest. There were the usual preliminary delays, and the trial was six months later."

"Did Clark make a motion for a change of judge?"

"Not that I recall," Broom replied. "And I'm certain I'd have remembered it. Are you onto something, George?"

"Maybe. Listen, one other thing. You looked at the news reports around the time of the arrest and trial. Was there ever anything about Boller himself, about his appointment to the bench, any hint of a black mark on his character?"

"No. But in the transcript, when Clark's on the stand, there are several notations that discussions were held off the record."

"Hmm. Well, thanks, Broom. By the way, do you know where Meyer is?"

"Home, I'd imagine."

"Okay. Thanks a lot. See you tomorrow."

Kelso hung up and called Meyer's house. He was there, sounding surly.

"What the hell do you want, Kelso? Can't I have a minute's peace when I'm off duty?"

"I just wanted to know if you found an apartment for the key."

"Not yet."

"Have you checked all the addresses?"

"Who do you think I am, Kelso? Superman? Those apartments are scattered all over the city. I'll finish 'em tomorrow."

"I was just curious. And did you get a ballistics or an autopsy report on Marilyn Strauss?"

"The bullet was a .38. They dug it out of her bedroom wall. According to the autopsy, it went in the back of her head and out the front, just like with the Boller broad. She died about five-thirty this morning. You can read it tomorrow, for yourself. Satisfied?"

"Thanks, Meyer. Have a nice evening."

Meyer muttered something and hung up.

Smith walked into the room and asked: "Well, are we playing chess, or do you plan to call fifty other people?" He had taken off his suit and tie and was in blue jeans, an old sweater, and Western boots.

"I'd rather not play tonight, if you don't mind."

"What?"

"Things are fitting together. Let's go have a talk with Judge Boller."

"Not tonight, surely?"

"No, wait, maybe you're right. Maybe I need a little more information before I talk to him. Damn, I wish Meyer had done all those addresses."

The phone rang. "Hello?" He realized he'd just answered Smith's phone and added: "Smith's residence."

"This is Stanley, George."

"Yes?"

"I just got off the phone with someone in the warden's office at the state reformatory. I thought you might be interested to know that Donald Clark was released two weeks ago, December 31, to 1423 Hedley Street, Apartment 12B."

"That's very interesting," Kelso said, quickly writing it down.

"Also, I just found something I'd noted from Clark's presentence investigation report."

"Go ahead." Kelso glanced at Smith, who was puffing at a cigarette and scowling.

Broom said, "At the time of Clark's arrest, he was working as a bank clerk and living at the same address, 1423 Hedley Street, in a different apartment, number 9A."

Kelso's pulse jumped, then he frowned. "Yes?"

"Yes. He'd been living there for two years. Before that, he was in law school, at the local university, and living at Colonial Estates Apartments, 926 North Central Avenue." Broom paused, then added: "Apartment 217."

Kelso's pulse jumped again, and this time he didn't frown. He could tell from Broom's tone that the plump young detective was smiling broadly. Kelso himself felt too stunned to reply immediately. It was as if a huge weight had been lifted from his chest. He drew in a deep breath and let it out very slowly before asking:

"Are you absolutely certain of the apartment number?"

"Absolutely."

"Who's got the key now? You, or Meyer?"

"Meyer has the original, but we made a copy so I could check my share of the addresses."

"Great. Listen, could you meet Smith and me at the Colonial Estates Apartments in, say, half an hour?"

"I'll leave right away," Broom said.

Kelso could hear a rather shrill female voice in the background—the notorious Mrs. Broom, who was always bothersome about what her husband did after normal duty hours. There was the muffled sound of a hand covering the mouthpiece, then it was lifted and Broom said:

"I'll meet you there in thirty minutes."

He must have won the argument.

When Kelso hung up, Smith was glaring at him, his cold blue eyes floating just beneath his heavy upper lids. "Kelso, what the hell's going on? Why are we meeting Broom at some apartment at eight-thirty at night?"

"Haven't you guessed?"

"You're not talking about number 217, surely?"

"Broom found it. It was in the presentencing report."

Smith stood up. ''Jesus Christ. And Meyer didn't look there first? Since he still didn't know of an apartment numbered 217 as of today, two days after the murder, I assumed he'd at least looked in the obvious places.''

''Well, apparently not. But Broom did. That's the nine hundred block of North Central.''

''I know the place. Big brick building, kind of rundown. Not a great neighborhood. About four blocks south of the hospital. So we're not playing chess tonight?''

''This may really be it,'' Kelso said. ''And by the way, here's another thing. Broom checked with the reformatory—''

''I was planning to do that tomorrow,'' Smith said.

''Well, Broom did it tonight. And found that they released Clark two weeks ago, but not to the 217 address. I wrote it down. We need to see if he's there.''

''Don't get yourself all excited, Kelso. None of this may amount to anything.''

''I think it will.''

They waited five minutes, then put on their coats and left Smith's apartment. Outside, it was cold, and snow fell in small sparkling flakes. Already the yards and sidewalks had a clean white cover over the grime that had recently accumulated, and the streets looked frosted with powdered sugar.

When they arrived at the address twenty minutes later, Broom's dark blue Toyota was already parked in front. They climbed out of Kelso's VW and entered the building.

Thirty-five

Broom was waiting for them in the lobby, sitting in an upholstered armchair with his overcoat unbuttoned, looking, at 9 P.M. after a full day's work, as fresh and energetic as a child. The lobby was a large square with a high ceiling, tiled floor, paneled walls, one of those banks of mailboxes with little glass windows and combination locks, and a closed door marked MANAGER. Broom got up, smiling, and said:

"Hello, George. Karl."

Smith nodded, and Kelso said: "Sorry we're late. I was trying to give you some extra time."

"I left right away, and there wasn't much traffic."

"Well, let's see if we can find the manager."

"Hardly likely, is it?" Smith asked. "At 9 P.M.?"

"Sometimes there's a night manager," Kelso said, and went over to the door. He knocked a few times, but nobody answered.

"Here's something," Smith said. "A note, here by the mailboxes. 'After six, see Mr. Simms, Assistant Manager, Apartment 108.' "

"Let's go, then." Kelso led the way down a long hall, past numbered doors. It was dimly lit and smelled of rancid wax. Faint music could be heard coming from one of the apartments. They paused at number 108 and Smith used a brass knocker. After a couple of minutes, the door opened a few inches and a thin, fiftyish man peered out at them. He had thin gray hair, a thick black mustache, and a tired look around his pale gray eyes.

"Yes?"

"Police," Smith said, showing his I.D. folder. "We'd like to ask you a few questions. Can we come inside?"

"Well . . ."

"Are you Mr. Simms, the assistant manager?"

"Yes, sir."

"Good. It won't take a minute."

Kelso smiled warmly at the man. "Just a routine investigation of one of your former tenants, Mr. Simms. All right?"

Mr. Simms backed away and let them inside. The room was small, neat, adequately furnished, with a masculine look about it: dark colors, no frills, simple and functional. Classical music came from stereo speakers—something by Brahms, Kelso thought.

"A former resident?" Mr. Simms asked. He seemed nervous.

Kelso noticed a small black-and-white cat lying at one end of the sofa, staring at them with big green eyes. It seemed very relaxed. Mr. Simms, he decided, must be a nice man.

"Donald Clark," Smith said. "It would've been over ten years ago, maybe twelve or thirteen. He lived in number 217."

"I've been here seventeen years now," Mr. Simms said. "But people come and go. There aren't many of us left, many who've been here long. I can't recollect any Donald Clark." He frowned. "Donald Clark. No, I'm sorry."

"Do you have an index file or anything?" Kelso asked.

"We'd appreciate it," Broom said, smiling, "if you could check for us."

"Well, if you'll come along to the office . . . but I can't promise how far back the records go. And I'm only the assistant manager."

They left Mr. Simms's apartment and followed him back to the lobby. He used a big brass key to unlock the door marked MANAGER.

"Mr. Purvis is the actual manager," he said, opening the door and turning on a light. "Let's see. Here's the file." He pulled out the top drawer of a green metal cabinet. "Clark. Clark. Should be right here . . . Donald Clark?"

"That's right," Kelso said, and held his breath.

"Donald Clark." Mr. Simms pulled out a beige folder. "Moved in on August 27, 1973. Moved out on August 26, 1976. Three years."

"And," Smith asked, "what was the apartment number?"

Mr. Simms hesitated in the act of replacing the file folder, turned his head to peer at Smith, and said: "Why, 217, of course."

Kelso let out his breath. "Is anyone renting that apartment now, Mr. Simms?"

"Hmm." The assistant manager opened a desk drawer and looked inside a small box containing three-by-five cards. "It's vacant." He closed the drawer. "Want to rent it? Good rates, by the month or the half year."

"We'd like to see it, if you don't mind," Kelso said. For some reason his pulse rate had quickened. He thought of something else. "Before we go, do you have a way of knowing whether Donald Clark turned in his apartment key when he moved out?"

Mr. Simms frowned and pulled out the metal file drawer again, found the folder, squinted, and said: "He was assessed a five-dollar fee for losing his door key." He glanced up. "Anything else?"

"We'll see the apartment now, please."

It was on the second floor. Everything seemed dark and musty. The door to 217 had a brass knocker. Mr. Simms used a key and they followed him inside.

The apartment was furnished with inexpensive but solid pieces. There was a large square living room, a small kitchen, a bedroom with a double bed, and a bath with sink, toilet, and shower. Dust lay everywhere. The windows looked out onto an alley; snow fell past the panes.

Other than the dust, however, everything seemed neat and fairly clean.

The closets were empty, as were the dresser and bureau drawers and the kitchen and bathroom cabinets.

Kelso wandered around for a while, then could stand it no longer.

"Broom, could I have that key?"

"Certainly."

Broom handed it to him, a copy in lightweight metal, bright blue for some reason. Smith and Broom watched. Mr. Simms watched, too. Kelso stepped to the door, drew in a deep breath, let it out, and inserted the blue key into the lock.

It went all the way in.

He turned it.

The bolt moved out, into the locked position.

He turned it the other way, and the bolt receded.

He took the key out again and sighed heavily, looking at Broom's smile and Smith's icy blue eyes.

"Thanks very much, Mr. Simms," he said.

"So, did you fellas want to rent the apartment?"

"I'm sorry. Not just now."

Mr. Simms locked up again and they all went back downstairs. At the assistant manager's door they waited while he unlocked it and turned to face them.

"Thanks for your help," Kelso said.

"Yes," Broom said. "Thanks very much."

"Is this Donald Clark fella in some kind of trouble?" Mr. Simms asked, a worried look in his watery eyes.

"It's just a routine check," Smith said.

"Well, you fellas take it easy," Mr. Simms told them, and went in and closed his door.

They walked down the hall to the lobby and out into the cold darkness of the evening. Snow fell steadily.

"We've got him," Kelso said.

Thirty-six

Since Sheila Terman had worked the afternoon shift at the B & P, she knocked off at 9 P.M., said goodbye to Eddie the bartender, and went home. She was tired, her feet and the muscles of her calves hurt from standing and walking, and her nose was stuffy from all the smoke. In addition, she was starved. Her plan was to fix herself a nice soft-boiled egg, two pieces of raisin toast, a bowl of peaches with cream, and a glass of white wine. Then, after a long hot shower, she would lie on the sofa in her robe, have another glass of wine, and watch a movie on TV.

With all this in mind, she unlocked her apartment door, went inside, closed and locked the door, flipped on the lights, and turned around.

A man sat in one of her living room chairs, watching her.

Sheila froze.

She recognized him at once. Tall, slender, brown hair, brown eyes, very broad shoulders, a rather sneering expression on his wide mouth. His hair fell down over his forehead, not in any stylish way, but as though uncombed. Everything about him looked slovenly—his tattered wool sweater, ragged jeans, beat-up shoes, faded nylon jacket. She even noticed that the collar of his shirt was frayed. He grinned, and she saw his uneven teeth.

His name was Donald Clark.

She found her voice and said, scowling: "What the hell are *you* doing here? How'd you get in?"

He laughed, a harsh mirthful sound. "I broke out one of your bedroom windows. It was easy."

"You can't do that. It's breaking and entering."

He just laughed at her.

She could feel her heart pounding heavily, and realized that she was frightened. She thought about Marilyn, and Judge Boller's wife, each of them with a bullet in the back of the head, and thought she could discern a bulge in one of Donald's jacket pockets. He seemed very relaxed, sitting back in the chalr with his legs crossed and his long pale hands dangling loosely off the arms of the chair.

She stood by the door, trying to think what to do. She could unlock the door and run out, but he might catch her before she got very far along the corridor. She could brazen it out and see what he wanted, maybe stall for enough time to get to a kitchen knife.

"What do you want, Donald?" Her voice was high.

"I just thought I'd drop by and see how you were," he said. "You know, after ten years in the reformatory, a guy enjoys seeing his friends again. You. And Marilyn." He grinned. "So how are you, Sheila?"

"Listen, Donald, you'd better get out of here. My boyfriend'll be here any minute, and—"

"No he won't. Your boyfriend's Eddie, the bartender over at the B & P, and he's there right now, working, tending bar, and he won't get off till midnight. And this is Thursday, and Eddie never comes to see you on Thursday. You can take a bath and wash your hair and watch TV and go to bed early."

How could he possibly know all that? Her heartbeat quickened, she felt herself beginning to tremble.

"Listen, Donald—"

"Shut up!" His demeanor changed suddenly. The grin vanished. His eyes darkened, narrowed, became threatening. He put a hand into his jacket pocket and stood up. "You bitch," he said. "You helped them put me away."

"No, I didn't. I—"

"Boller bought himself some help, didn't he, Sheila? He bought two cops. He bought Marilyn. And he bought you."

He's going to kill me, she thought, feeling the panic starting to build low in her guts and work its way up into her chest and throat. Her scalp tingled and little shivers started running over her shoulders and face and arms. He's going to kill me, she thought.

"That's a lie," she tried, putting everything into it she had. "Nobody bought me, Donald."

"Bullshit! You're lying again, right now. You know you lied, Sheila." He took a step toward her. His hand was still in his jacket pocket. "You set me up. Marilyn came over to my place. Your little slut girlfriend. Know what she did? She drank wine with me, and made out with me, and tried to talk me into the bedroom. But we stayed in the living room, Sheila, we never got to the bedroom, because I wasn't in love with her, and I wasn't about to climb into the rack with some crazy sixteen-year-old high school girl, not when I already knew she was sleeping with a law professor named Henry Boller. I wasn't nuts, Sheila."

"But, Marilyn told me—"

"Marilyn didn't tell you shit!" He advanced toward her across the living room floor, his tennis shoes muffled on the shag carpeting. He moved halfway across the floor, then stopped again. Both hands in his jacket pockets, he glared and spoke in a kind of snarl. "You and Marilyn already had your stories straight. You told them exactly what Boller paid you to tell them. When those cops came in, Marilyn *let* them in. And we were in the living room, and I had my clothes on. *All* my clothes. And they hauled me downtown anyway and booked me and told everybody they'd found us in bed."

"Donald . . ." She could think of nothing to say. She shook her head and felt tears start to burn her eyes. Everything blurred. She blinked.

"Then you lied to the prosecutor, Sheila," he said. "When they asked you about it, you told 'em what you'd been paid to say—that Marilyn told you all about how I screwed her in my apartment that night. The same lie Marilyn told on the witness stand." He watched her for several seconds, as she stood trembling and unable to speak; then suddenly his mood seemed to shift again, and he grinned. He found his cigarettes, lit one with a match, puffed smoke, and tossed the match into an ashtray.

"I'll tell you something," he said, in a strange and quavery voice. "I talked to Boller before the trial, and during the trial, and after the trial. I reminded him of what good friends we'd been, when I was in his criminal law class. Justice. You know, he always used to talk about justice in there, how important it was for us to keep our heads as lawyers, keep our eyes focused always on justice." He laughed. "I reminded him of how I used to do him favors, like lending him my apartment key so he could cheat on his wife, the precious Barbara Boller."

"Donald—"

"You know what he used to do, Sheila? When everybody thought what a wonderful couple he and Barbara made, how pretty and poised she was and how loving and wonderful he was? All that time, he was using my key, my apartment, to shack up with young girls. Young girls, Sheila, just like you and Marilyn. Young whores."

She began to hope. Maybe he'd only come here to lecture her. After all, it had been Marilyn who'd actually testified at his rape trial, Marilyn who'd actually signed the criminal complaint and made her sworn statement against him. Sheila's only sin had been not coming forward with the truth. And even if she had, would anyone have believed her? In the face of Marilyn's statement and the reports of those two cops?

"Donald, there wasn't anything I could've done. I was only—"

"Shut up!" The grin left. His face clouded over again. He put one hand back inside a jacket pocket; with the other hand he crushed out his cigarette. "Sheila the bitch," he said. "I knew you were a bitch right from the start. And I was right."

She'd never make it to the kitchen. He had her blocked off. Her only chance was to reach behind, unlock the door, get into the hall, make for the building entrance, yell for help. It was only a little after nine-thirty on a Thursday night—surely someone would be around to hear, to help her. This was Clairmont City, not New York. Somebody would help her.

"You know how long ten years is, Sheila? In the state reformatory? You ought to try it sometime. I had time to think about it, and plan it. You know who killed Boller? And your bitch girlfriend Marilyn?"

She was starting to cry. That alone distressed her; she hadn't wanted to let him see her cry. She hated herself for being weak. But her fear was too much for her to handle. Tears wet her cheeks as she reached back, fumbled for the doorknob, tried to find the lock.

"No, I don't . . . please, Donald . . . don't hurt me . . ."

"Lying bitch," he snapped. He started toward her.

She tried to scream, but fingers around her throat cut off the sound. He pulled her from the door, and she was able to be surprised at his strength. Sobbing, she tried to claw at him, but her fingers flailed at nothing. He had his fingers tightly around her throat, making it almost impossible for her to breathe, and now he gripped her right wrist and twisted her arm around behind her back, sending pain shooting up into her shoulder.

He pulled her into the bedroom, and it occurred to her that he might be going to rape her first, as some sort of ironic revenge, taking from her what they'd accused him of taking from Marilyn. She was shoved facedown onto her bed, and felt a pillow being pressed down against the back of her neck.

His hand left her throat; she caught her breath and thought: This is silly, he can't suffocate me this way, with the pillow behind my head.

Then she realized what he was doing, and tried to throw herself off the bed, just as the noise came . . .

Thirty-seven

"We've got to check out the current address for Clark," Kelso said, getting into the VW and starting it up. He had to get out again and scrape snow from the windows. Back inside, he added: "But I don't suppose he'll still be there."

"Not if he has any sense at all," Smith said. "On the other hand, most criminals have no sense at all."

"I think it's time for another talk with Boller," Kelso said.

"You're probably right."

Broom had gotten into his Toyota and headed for home, back to the wife who had become irate at his having gone out to pursue an important investigation. Kelso drove north, wipers clacking at the snow, and in twenty-five minutes they arrived at the Wadding Way address. This time they pulled right into the judge's driveway; the time for pretension and secrecy had passed.

"What if he refuses to see us?" Smith asked.

"Threaten to take him downtown to one of those little rooms," Kelso said.

They knocked at the judge's front door. In the darkness of the yard, only dimly illuminated by the nearest streetlight, all the tracks from the murder investigation were slowly being covered over by new white snow, as though a pen-and-ink drawing were being erased.

The door opened.

"Yes? Oh—it's you."

"Evening, your honor," Kelso said. "I realize it's late, but could we see you for a few minutes?"

Boller frowned. He was in a dark gray suit and white shirt, but his collar was open and he'd taken off his tie. Black-and-white stubble was visible on the smooth paleness of his jaws. His bushy eyebrows and thick mustache made three black rectangles on his narrow face.

"What's it about? Can't it wait?"

"It's about Donald Clark," Kelso said.

Boller shook his head. "I see no need to discuss Donald Clark."

"Remember that key we found lying on your wife's body?" Smith asked. "With the number 217 on it?"

"Yes? So?"

"It belonged to Clark." Smith's voice was hard. "It was the key to the apartment he let you use, when you were cheating on your wife."

Boller's eyes narrowed. After a moment he said gruffly: "I expect you'd better come inside."

In the judge's living room, a log flamed in the fireplace, snapping and popping. One lamp was lit, over a chair; next to it, a book lay open on a side table.

Boller stood in the middle of the room with his hands behind his back and scowled without offering them a chair.

"Now, suppose you tell me what this is all about," he said.

"From what we've been able to find out," Kelso began, "when you were teaching law and Donald Clark was a student in one of your classes, and you were already married to Barbara, you were seeing other women."

Boller's face was impassive.

"You borrowed Clark's apartment key, number 217, and took young women there. And in return, you gave him an A in criminal law."

The log shifted with a loud thud. Kelso found that his nerves were on edge. The flames made weird shadows jump around the room.

Smith began pacing restlessly.

"Go on," Boller said.

"A year or so later, when you were up for an appointment to the criminal bench, Clark came to see you. I'm not sure of the exact details, but probably he threatened to go to the press about the key matter, unless you paid him a certain amount of money or did other favors for him. We know he eventually flunked out of law school. Maybe he thought you could get him back in. At any rate, you refused. Instead, you had him arrested for raping Marilyn Strauss."

"He *did* rape Marilyn Strauss," Boller snapped. "And therefore he was arrested and charged. How could I possibly have had anything to do with that?"

Smith paced. The fire crackled. Kelso wiped his palms on his corduroy trousers and said:

"You convinced Marilyn, whom you were seeing at the time, to go with Donald to his apartment, and to try and seduce him. You convinced two patrolmen to enter his place that night at eleven, when they were to have been in bed. The police officers went in and arrested him. Sheila Terman, Marilyn's best friend, knew about it, knew Donald had been set up, but you convinced her not to say anything."

"Convinced!" Boller sneered. "You keep saying I convinced them. I convinced two policemen, I convinced Marilyn Strauss, I convinced Sheila Terman. How did I manage to convince all these people?"

"I don't know," Kelso said quietly. "Maybe you paid them."

"You stand here accusing me in my own house, and you use the word 'maybe'?"

"Yes, sir. But I'm sure of what happened, even if I'm not quite sure yet how it happened."

"Go on," Boller said dryly. "I like a good story."

"Donald Clark was tried in your courtroom, found guilty, and sentenced by you to ten years in the state reformatory. About two weeks ago he was released, came here, and started watching your house. He noticed that every night at ten o'clock you walked your dog. Tuesday night this week, he hid by the evergreen tree, where the dog always went, and waited for you. But you and Barbara had an argument that night, and for some reason she walked the dog herself. It was dark in the hall and she put on your coat by accident . . ."

Kelso paused. Something had occurred to him as he spoke, something jarring. But it was only a possibility.

"Yes?" Boller said, glowering.

"By accident," Kelso continued. "But probably it wouldn't have mattered. She was a tall dark figure in a fur hat, walking the dog in the snow, and as far as Donald Clark was concerned, it was you. He fired, trying to kill you, and killed her instead."

"Fascinating," Boller said. His eyes were like hard coals; it was becoming difficult for Kelso to meet his stare.

"Yes, sir. But before Clark left, he made a gesture, a kind of private signal that he knew nobody else would understand, except possibly for Marilyn Strauss and Sheila Terman. He still had his old apartment key, the one he'd let you use, and he tossed it down onto what he thought was your dead body, as a kind of spiteful goodbye."

"Yes?"

"But he wasn't finished yet. He went to Marilyn Strauss's apartment early this morning. Apparently he simply knocked and she let him in. He took her back to her bedroom and shot her. After all, she'd falsely accused him of rape."

Boller smiled, a kind of ironic grimace, turned, and walked over to the fire. He stood for a while with his pale hands clasped behind his back, gazing into the flames, then turned and glared at Kelso.

"Everything you've said is tripe. Donald Clark was arrested by two Clairmont City police officers who acted on an anonymous tip to the effect that Clark was in there having sexual relations with a minor, which constitutes statutory rape. They had probable cause to enter, and they did. They discovered Clark and this Marilyn person, in bed, naked, performing a sexual act. The young woman agreed to prosecute and Clark was duly arrested, charged, tried, convicted, and sentenced. Nobody convinced anybody to do anything. It was a straightforward crime."

He paused. Kelso said nothing. Smith paced.

"It's quite possible," the judge said, "that Clark got out of jail and shot my wife, and possibly Marilyn Strauss, out of simple hatred. It's common for criminals to threaten the prosecutor who charged them, the judge who tried and convicted and sentenced them, the victim who complained against them, even the attorney who defended them. But I convinced no one of anything. I never took women to Donald Clark's apartment. And it's slander for you to say otherwise. I was never *in* Donald Clark's apartment."

"That's a lie," Smith said quietly.

Boller's head shot around. He squinted at Smith.

"I'll have your badge for that!"

"No you won't," Smith told him. "We talked to Sheila Terman, and she told us the whole thing. She caved in, Judge. All about you and Marilyn, how you were seeing Marilyn every Thursday night. Your secretary told us the same thing. And Sheila told us all about Clark's apartment, number 217, and the key. We know the whole damn thing."

"You can't possibly—"

"Kelso and I just came from Clark's old apartment. We had the key we found on your wife's body. The key fit Clark's door, number 217. Just like Sheila Terman said."

Kelso watched the muscles working in the sides of Boller's face. He seemed to be chewing, or biting. He had gone even more pale than usual, and his thin fingers worked at themselves, twisting and pulling.

Then he said: "Think what you like. You don't have a gram of proof. It's Sheila's word against mine." He moved away from the fireplace, back to the center of the room, and glared down at Kelso. "And, in any event, it's nothing to do with me. Not now, not at this point. My wife's dead, Marilyn Strauss is dead. I don't understand why you're telling me any of this. I deny it emphatically, but it's pointless for you to come here and tell it to me."

"Not pointless, your honor," Kelso told him. "I'm sorry, but it's not pointless at all."

"Then what's the *point?*"

"We're trying to save your life," Kelso said quietly.

"Me? My life? And exactly how do you propose doing that?"

"Clark was after you Tuesday night. You may not be willing to admit the reasons for it, but it's a fact that he came here and shot someone he thought was you."

Judge Boller frowned, turned away, and went back to stare at the fire.

Kelso inhaled deeply, watching the judge's hunched shoulders and broad back, and said loudly:

"It was you he wanted, Judge Boller. He tried to murder you. He succeeded in murdering Marilyn. And he'll be back. He's not going to give up. He'll be back here, to finish the job."

Boller turned around. He seemed to have relaxed slightly. His voice was lower, less hard:

"If that's all it is, then you can stop your worrying. This house is burglarproof. Don't you think I've had attempts on my life before? No one can get inside here. The windows all have bulletproof glass. The doors are steel. There are two separate alarm systems, with backup power supplies. I sleep like a baby. Once I'm inside and locked up for the night, I'm completely safe."

"You're forgetting one thing," Smith said.

"And what's that?"

"Your dog." His cold blue eyes watched the judge. His lips turned upward into a slight smile. "You can't stay here twenty-four hours a day. You've got to walk your dog."

Boller shrugged. "Well, there are never guarantees in this world. I could be hit by a car, or a building could collapse on me. We all run daily risks."

"We're talking about Donald Clark," Kelso said.

"I'm tired." Boller took a step toward the hall door. "There's nothing else to talk about. I'll show you out."

"Wait," Kelso said. "We want you to help us."

"Help you? Help you do what?"

"Catch Donald Clark."

"You're a police officer," Boller said. "That's your job, not mine. This way, please." He walked toward the door.

"You owe it to your wife," Kelso said.

Boller halted, turned, and glared. "And what the devil do you mean by *that?*"

"You're the reason she's dead," Kelso replied, very quietly. And stood waiting for the outburst, hands clinched hard at his sides.

Thirty-eight

Boller looked at Kelso for a moment, then crossed to his armchair and sat down in it. Leaning back, he folded his arms over his chest.

"I hope you have a good education, Sergeant Kelso, because tomorrow morning I'm going to have a talk with the chief of police, and by ten o'clock you'll be out on the street, looking for a job."

Smith snapped: "You make me sick!"

Boller's eyes flickered. "You have no right—"

"Just shut your goddamned mouth," Smith told him. "What a bastard you are. No, just shut up till I've finished. First you cheat on your wife, with sluts from some bar. You probably committed the same statutory rape Clark was accused of. Then you frame the poor sap, because he might tell the papers he let you use his apartment and you might not get to be a judge. You bribe two cops, who obviously didn't deserve to be cops anyway, and you bribe that slut Marilyn and her friend the waitress, and the sap goes to jail for ten years."

"You can't—"

"Shut up, I said. And while the sap's in jail, you keep right on cheating your wife with this topless dancer slut, Marilyn, and probably lots of others we don't know about. Then you sit here and deny it, and you're lying out your ass, and you've got the nerve to threaten my partner with his job."

Smith stepped closer to the judge's chair and stared down at him, his eyes like ice. The judge's mouth opened, but closed again. His face was red.

"Do you have even a shred of decency in you? I've always thought big shots like you were corrupt, but are you really that far gone? That you'd sit here, with your wife barely in the ground, and lie, and lie, and lie? Is that all it means to you, your precious oath of office, your wedding vows, your existence as a human being on this planet?"

Kelso felt a little amazed. Normally Smith refrained from making speeches, but obviously Boller had gotten to him. Now, he thought, taking in a deep breath, we can both look for work. He glanced at Boller.

The judge seemed to have withered. He sat in his chair, arms no longer crossed, hands loosely together on his lap, shoulders slumped, head slightly bowed. For a while, there was only the crackle of the fire and, from somewhere in the house, the ticking of a clock. Then Boller spoke in a low gruff voice, frowning down at his hands.

"You gentlemen don't know how it is. You don't know what it is to scrape and claw and try to succeed. You don't know what the competition is. You seem to have some kind of damned idealistic notion that it's a fairy tale. It's not. Everybody out there is scheming, conniving, waiting to stab you in the back. It's really the jungle they all say it is. After a while, you see too much, you experience too much, and you come to understand that the road to power's got a price, and you've got to decide whether or not to pay it." He paused, opened his mouth, shook his head. "I'll never forget everything that was said in this room tonight, but I will purport to forget it. As far as the rest of the world's concerned, it never happened. And you'll both do the same. No one will know."

"And you'll help us catch Donald Clark?" Kelso asked.

The judge looked up at him, but said nothing.

"First," Kelso said softly, "you promised to love your wife and to take care of her. Then you took women to Clark's apartment. You sent an innocent man to prison for ten years. You slept with Marilyn Strauss every Thursday night while your wife thought you were working late. Then you sent your wife out to be shot by Clark."

Boller sat motionless, as if in a trance. But Kelso could see him starting to waver. He was wringing his thin hands now, and his jaw muscles were working again. The fight had left his eyes.

"Judge, wasn't there ever a time when you loved your wife? When Barbara meant something to you?" Kelso kept his voice soft. "Even at the end, even that last night, when you argued, didn't you feel something for her? And didn't she love you, and trust you?"

Boller licked his thin lips. His eyes had become watery; he kept blinking them.

"It was because of you," Kelso said, "that she died. You sent her out there that night, in your coat, to be shot down by the man who wanted you dead because you used him. That should've been you out there, lying dead in the snow. That should've been your brains and blood. Don't you owe her anything at all?"

The clock seemed louder. But time seemed frozen.

"Your honor?"

When Boller finally replied, his voice was gruff again, but low, barely audible. Not looking at either of them, he said:

"What do you want me to do?"

Thirty-nine

"Smith and I think," Kelso said, "that Donald Clark will definitely make another attempt to kill you. Probably he knows he can't get inside, or he'd have done it the first time. You always walk the dog at 10 P.M., and the dog always goes to that big evergreen tree out in back, and that's a perfect setup for Clark."

"He's bound to try the same thing again," Smith agreed.

Kelso felt pleased. He and Smith hadn't discussed this in so many words, but obviously they had both arrived at the same conclusion. Creative police work, he thought.

Boller frowned. "But won't he expect you to look for him this time?"

"No," Smith said. "For two reasons. One, he doesn't know we suspect him. Two, we're going to help him a little, and announce an arrest tomorrow."

Kelso glanced at Smith, who smiled briefly and nodded. Kelso nodded back. He felt good. It was like playing cards with a partner who knew how you played. The two of you could predict each other's moves without saying anything.

"An arrest," the judge said, looking confused. "An arrest?"

"Sure," Kelso said. "We'll have a press conference, pull somebody in from the street, make everyone think we've found the killer. Nobody will be permitted to talk to the suspect." It was something they had done before, to lure a criminal into the open. Occasionally, it even worked.

"Clark'll start to think he's home-free," Smith said. "He'll feel confident. He'll watch your house again, he won't see any cops, and one night when you take the dog out for its walk, he'll have another try at you."

Kelso nodded. "It'll mean, your honor, that we'll have to stay here with you, until he makes his move."

"Here?" The black eyes narrowed. "Why?"

"We can't let him see us coming and going. And we've got to be here when he tries anything."

"Don't worry," Smith told him, "we won't get in your way. We'll be as quiet as little mice. You won't even know we're here. You'll have to buy a few extra groceries, of course. I myself don't eat that much. But Kelso, on the other hand . . ."

"The Department'll pay for it," Kelso said. "Well, Judge?"

"I don't know." He frowned again. "This is unheard of. Besides, he could try to get me someplace else. My office, going or coming from the Municipal Building, a restaurant—"

"Life's full of chances," Smith said.

"For my money," Kelso said, "he'll try it again right here. The next time there's a good fresh snow. I think he likes the little mystery created by the absence of his footprints."

"How'd he manage it?" Boller asked. "Not leave any tracks, I mean."

"He can fly," Smith said.

Boller scowled. Kelso started to say something, but the telephone rang. Boller picked it up.

"Boller speaking." He listened. "Yes, they're here. Just a moment." He held out the receiver to Kelso. "Someone named Meyer."

Kelso took the phone. "Meyer?"

"Kelso, where the hell've you been? You might tell somebody when you plan to go off and disappear like this. What the hell're you doing at that judge's place?"

"Talking," Kelso said blandly. "What's up?"

"I'll tell you what's up. You know that waitress, the blonde named Sheila Terman? From the B & P?"

"Sure."

"Well, she's dead. Bullet in the back of her head. Just like Barbara Boller and Marilyn Strauss."

"A .38?"

"They've just dug the bullet out of her bedroom mattress, but it looks like it. You wouldn't happen to know anything about this, would you?"

"It was Donald Clark," Kelso said.

"No kidding! You sound awfully damned sure of yourself, Kelso. Have you arrested him yet?"

"No. But we will." He told Meyer what had happened. When he hung up, he looked from Boller to Smith and said:

"Sheila Terman's been murdered. Same way as Marilyn. Obviously it was Clark." He sighed. The judge looked upset. "You're causing quite a little string of bodies, your honor."

Boller made no reply.

"I don't think Clark'll try anything yet. We're getting some new snow. He'll wait to see how much accumulates." Kelso began zipping up his parka. "Tomorrow morning we'll announce the arrest, and Smith and I'll move in with you. We'll plant an officer across the street with a good view of the evergreen tree. And you'll walk your dog every night."

"Sheila Terman," Boller said. He seemed to have lost his anger.

"See you tomorrow, Judge," Smith said.

"We'll meet at your office," Kelso told him.

Boller sat stiffly in his chair and nodded, looking tired. With a glance at Smith, Kelso shrugged and led the way into the hall and out of the house. It was 10:20 P.M., Thursday, January 14, and the snow was still falling.

Forty

That night Kelso watched an old jungle movie on TV and went to bed. The movie had been about natives and apes and some secret gold, and he dreamed about a golden monkey that was looking for lost bananas. Once he awoke in a sweat from some vague nightmare and remembered that he'd neglected to telephone Susan before turning in, but now it was too late. He went back to sleep.

When he awoke again, it was Friday, the sun was out, and he had a headache.

At the detective section he found a message on his desk. It was from Lieutenant Leill, in the form of a handwritten note from Meyer, whom Leill had called. The lieutenant was still out of town and would probably be back on Monday. By that time, Leill trusted, Kelso would have made an arrest in the Boller case.

Kelso lit his pipe and tossed the note into his trash can.

Smith came in, took off his coat, sat down, and looked at Kelso.

"You look like hell," he said, lighting a cigarette.

"I didn't sleep well last night."

"Second thoughts?"

"I don't know. It all bothers me. Last night it sounded perfectly logical, but this morning I'm not so sure. What if Clark never shows up again? What if he simply shoots Boller in a coffee shop?"

"What if Martians land and take over the country?" Smith said. "By the way, I've taken care of the arrest thing. We won't really have to arrest anybody after all. See what you think of this.'' He got up and handed Kelso a sheet of paper. It was a typed paragraph that read:

> Clairmont Police officials announced today the arrest of Herbert James Medford, on charges of murdering Mrs. Henry Boller, Miss Marilyn Strauss, and Miss Sheila Terman. Due to the unusually sensitive nature of the case, officials are unable to divulge specific information at this time, but Mr. Medford, who has a long police record, is being held without bail and the Department is confident that they have sufficient evidence for a grand jury indictment.

''That's outlandish,'' Kelso said, handing it back.

''Well, it's only a rough draft. It needs a little work.''

''Where'd you get the name Herbert James Medford?''

''I made it up.''

Kelso shook his head. ''Eventually the press will find out it's a lie.''

''And by then,'' Smith said, ''we'll have Donald Clark in custody.'' He got up. ''Come on, I'll buy you some breakfast. You look like you could use some.''

They went across the street to a coffee shop. It was now nine-thirty on the morning of the fifteenth. The sky was clear. Most of the recent snow had melted.

''Things are going wrong already,'' Kelso said, sipping coffee after a bite of yeast doughnut. ''This will probably be one of those unusual winters with no more snow.''

''You worry too much.'' Smith was eating a cheese Danish with hot tea. ''I saw the extended outlook this morning, and they're calling for a 70 percent chance of measurable snow by Saturday.''

''Since when are they ever right?''

''Don't worry about it,'' Smith said.

''What if Boller changes his mind—''

''Will you stop it? You're driving me nuts.''

Kelso sighed. After a while he said: "I think I've figured out how it was done."

Smith looked up. "What?"

"How Clark did it, without leaving his prints in the snow."

"Are you serious?"

"Yes. I watched a late movie last night. It was something about a jungle. Did you ever read about the famous experiment some psychologist did, in which a hungry monkey has to find a way to get a banana that's dangling just out of reach, outside its cage?"

"No. Sounds like cruelty to animals to me."

"Well, it's a famous experiment."

"Obviously," Smith said.

"The monkey has a stick in its cage. After a while, it gives up trying to reach the banana with its hands and tries the stick, which is just long enough. It uses it to pull the banana close enough to the bars to grab it."

"That's really fascinating, Kelso. But what the hell's it got to do with your jungle movie, and with the case? You think Clark murdered Mrs. Boller with a banana?"

"I think he murdered her with a stick."

Smith stared at him in amazement. Then, gradually, comprehension spread over his pale thin features.

"By God, Kelso, I think you've got something."

"I think so, too. The only thing I don't understand is why Clark would go to all that trouble to murder Boller, then simply walk in and shoot Marilyn and Sheila in their apartments."

"Maybe just to create confusion," Smith said. "Make us look for two different killers. The question is, will he use the same method again, to try and get Boller?"

"I have a feeling he will." Kelso finished his doughnut. "Mainly because, if it were me, I'd do it. I'd be having fun with it, thinking how puzzled the cops would be about the key and the absence of tracks in the snow. I think I'd try exactly the same thing again."

"He should be good and worried by now," Smith said.

"He knows we've got that key, and we might be able to trace it back to his old apartment."

"Hopefully, he won't be so worried when he reads about the arrest."

They finished their snacks and went back across to the Municipal Building. It was 11 A.M., and still very clear.

Seconds after they sat down at their desks, Meyer and Broom came in, and Kelso explained what he and Smith had planned.

"That's the most absurd thing I ever heard of," Meyer said.

"I kind of like it," Broom said.

"I'm not going to give my official approval for a lie to the press," Meyer went on. "It's out of the question."

"You don't have to approve it," Smith told him. "Kelso's handling the whole thing, in Leill's absence."

"I outrank both of you," Meyer snapped.

"So sue us," Smith said.

Meyer scowled. "You guys do what you want. But just remember, if you screw it up, it wasn't me, I didn't know anything about it."

"We never told you," Kelso said. "You're not involved."

"Bet your ass," Meyer snapped, and stalked out of the room.

At four-thirty that afternoon, Henry Boller got into the driver's seat of his yellow Fleetwood Cadillac, started up the engine, and drove up the inclined ramp to the street. A large blanket had been spread over something bulky in the rear seat, but from outside the car it was not at all clear what was there. It simply looked like a blanket. He might have been taking home some old files.

Boller drove north in his usual manner and arrived at his house on Wadding Way at five minutes till five. He activated the automatic opener and the garage door slid up. The Cadillac eased quietly inside and the door shut. He killed the engine and got out, then opened the door to the house.

"You can come out now," he said, rather gruffly.

The blanket moved. Kelso and Smith crawled out from under it. They got their bags from the judge's trunk and followed him quickly inside the house. After making certain that all the drapes and curtains were drawn, Boller turned on the lights.

Kelso and Smith stood in the hall, holding their bags, looking a little sheepish. Boller frowned.

"Well," he said, "I suppose you may as well make yourselves comfortable."

"I hope it's a short stay," Kelso said.

Boller nodded. "So do I."

The two detectives carried their suitcases upstairs to a guest room and began to unpack. Outside the windows, the sun was setting, and clouds were starting to move in from the west. The forecast was for snow by midnight.

Kelso sat down on one of the twin beds and took out his pipe, while Smith placed his underwear neatly in a bureau drawer.

"By the way," Kelso said. "Meyer and Broom checked out Clark's current address. He wasn't there."

"Surprise, surprise," Smith murmured.

"I forgot to tell you earlier."

"Hmm."

"Well," Kelso said, "now we wait, I guess."

"Yep."

From downstairs, they could hear the yapping of the judge's dog.

Forty-one

Boller, it turned out, was not an especially gifted cook. Fortunately, though, he'd had the foresight to purchase a number of frozen dinners. That evening they had spinach lasagna and part of a chocolate cake Kelso had bought at a downtown bakery. Then they sat in the judge's living room, watching the fire.

Boller was under orders to do nothing unusual; he sat in an armchair, scowling at a book, while the little black poodle slept curled up at his feet. Kelso and Smith sat on the sofa and watched, Smith puffing at Kents and leafing through several news magazines, Kelso playing with his pipe and trying to work a crossword puzzle.

At one point, Kelso turned to Smith and asked: "What time do you have?"

"Quarter to seven. Why?"

"She'll expect me to call."

"Then maybe you'd better call her," Smith said. He gave Kelso a strange look and returned to his magazine.

Kelso got up and went to the kitchen, where one of the judge's telephones sat on a counter. He dialed the number and she answered on the third ring.

"Susan? It's me."

"George. Where are you? I tried to call."

"Sorry. Listen, I'm not going to be at home for a few days. Do you still have that extra key to my place?"

"Of course."

"Good. You wouldn't mind feeding my cat, would you?"

"Why? Are you up to something?"

He hesitated. Susan wouldn't tell anyone, but even a facial expression could give something away. He decided not to explain about the judge. "One of our witnesses has been threatened," he said. "Smith and I are staying with him for a while, until the suspect's been arraigned."

Silence. Could she tell he was lying by the tone of his voice on the phone? Then she said:

"I'll feed your cat. Be careful, George."

"I will. Thanks. There's nothing to worry about."

"I love you."

"Me too."

They hung up.

At nine o'clock Kelso went up to the guest room and brought down a shoe box, removed the lid, and took it over to Boller.

"Your honor?"

Boller frowned. "Yes? What is it?"

"When you go out with the dog tonight, put this on."

"What the devil is that?"

"An earplug and a radio receiver. Put the plug in your ear and the radio in your pocket."

"Hmm."

"In the dark, with your hat and scarf, it'll be practically invisible."

The receiver was about the size and shape of a small pocket calculator, and tuned to the frequency of Kelso's transmitter. It was the last thing he and Smith had dreamed up, just an hour before leaving in Boller's car.

"Why should I wear an earplug and listen to a radio?" the judge asked irritably.

"In case Donald Clark's out there," Kelso explained. "When you stand by the evergreen tree where your wife was shot, that's when he'll try for you. We want to catch him in the act, but before he gets you. When we see him start to make his move, I'll speak into this microphone."

He took a small object from his pocket and held it up. It looked like a thick silver pen. "I'll tell you to duck."

"To duck?"

"Yes, sir."

Smith chuckled.

"It's serious," Kelso said, with a frown at Smith. "I'll say 'Duck,' and immediately you hit the ground. Do you understand? Otherwise . . ."

The judge blinked and ran a thin white finger over his mustache. "Otherwise, I could be shot."

"Don't worry," Kelso said. "We've got somebody in a house across the street. We'll know when Clark's heading for the tree. All you have to do is duck when I tell you, and it'll go all right. Then we'll come out and get him."

"Won't he simply come out from behind the tree, then, and shoot me anyway?" Boller asked.

"It'll be hard for him to do that, sir. Wait a minute." Kelso trotted back upstairs, then came down again with a stick about the size of a yardstick but thicker and a few inches longer. There was a nail in one end. To the other end was attached his service revolver, bound with heavy wire.

"See this string running from the trigger to the nail at the other end?" Kelso asked. "This is how I think he killed your wife. He stood under the tree branches and simply extended some sort of stick or pole with a gun attached to the end, just like this. He poked it out until the gun was a couple of inches from the back of her head and . . ."

Kelso had already cocked the .38, which was empty. He pulled the string, and the hammer struck with a click.

"See?" Kelso said.

Boller stared. Smith chuckled faintly. Boller said:

"And you really think that's how he did it?"

"I can't think of any other way," Kelso said. "It had to've been something like this, or he'd have left footprints."

"I see." The judge gave him a long look, then put the

earplug in his left ear. He frowned, adjusted it, and took it out again. "I suppose I'll have to wear it," he said.

"Don't forget to duck," Smith told him. He seemed to find it all very funny.

Kelso took his gun and stick back upstairs.

At nine-thirty the judge opened the back door and looked up at the sky, then returned to the living room to report that the clouds had broken up and he could see stars here and there.

At three minutes till ten he inserted the earplug and shoved the radio receiver into his jacket pocket, put on his long dark overcoat, fur hat, scarf, and leather gloves, and put the leash on the poodle. He opened the front door.

Kelso and Smith went to stand in the dining room, and peered out the circular bay window. They heard the front door close and after a moment saw Boller come around the side of the house, the dog prancing at the end of its leash. The telephone rang.

Smith picked up the dining room extension. "Yes?"

The judge and the dog had reached the tree.

"Okay. I'll tell him." He hung up. "That was Broom. He and Meyer are in the house directly across from the alley, on Agnes Street. It's owned by a Mrs. Carpathian."

"I know all that," Kelso said impatiently. Mrs. Carpathian was a seventy-three-year-old widow who had agreed to allow Broom to stay with her for a few days, for official police surveillance. "What'd he say?"

"They've been watching the alley. They can see almost directly down its length. Nobody's been in it, and they don't think there's anybody in the tree."

"The dog's doing its duty now," Kelso said. And, in a moment: "They're coming back now." He held up his transmitter and spoke into it. "Hello, Judge Boller? Touch your hand to your hat if you can hear me."

Boller put his free hand on his Russian-style fur hat, then took it away again.

A few minutes later the front door opened and they heard the judge come inside with the dog.

"Why's Meyer over there with Broom?" Kelso asked, putting the transmitter in his pocket. "I thought he wasn't having anything to do with this."

"Apparently he changed his mind," Smith said dryly.

Boller came to the dining room door and looked in at them. "I'm going to bed now. If no one objects."

It was the end of the first day.

Forty-two

Two days later it was Sunday night, and Kelso went to bed in the judge's guest room in an irritable mood. It still had not snowed, the judge had walked his dog two more times, and nothing had happened. Kelso was beginning to feel like a prisoner, cooped up with Smith in Boller's house, staying away from the windows, eating frozen dinners warmed in a microwave oven. Moreover, he had neglected to bring his own pillow and was finding it almost impossible to get a decent night's sleep on the flimsy thing Boller had provided.

Monday morning they awoke to find the city in the grip of a heavy snow. A winter storm warning had been issued; two and a half inches had accumulated since midnight, and the weather bureau was calling for an additional three to six inches before sunset.

Boller drove his yellow Cadillac out of the garage and headed for his office. Smith and Kelso had the house to themselves, along with the little black poodle, who seemed to sleep a lot.

At 10 A.M. Meyer telephoned from the widow's house to ask how it was going.

"We're bored and hungry, that's how it's going," Smith said. "How did you imagine it was going?"

Kelso sucked at his pipe, which had gone out again.

"Well, it wasn't *my* idea," Smith said, and hung up.

The snow continued to fall.

By three in the afternoon, it had tapered to flurries, and when Boller arrived home again at five-forty-five it had quit. Approximately five new inches of snow lay over the pleasant and proper lawns of the well-to-do neighborhood. City plows had managed to clear a few of the main streets and would be out all night. Boller entered the living room and sank heavily into his armchair.

"It's a madhouse," he said. "Traffic's bumper to bumper."

"Let's check the radio transmitter again," Kelso said.

The judge inserted his earplug, reluctantly, and Kelso went upstairs and spoke into the microphone.

"Testing, testing," he said. And then: "A Volkswagen is a very good car." Then he trotted back down to the living room. The judge was just removing the earplug. "What'd you hear, your honor? Repeat it, please."

Boller frowned. "Testing, testing."

"Yes?"

He frowned harder. "Something about a Volkswagen's being a very good car."

"Ah," Kelso said.

Smith looked at the ceiling.

Meyer telephoned at seven-thirty to say that he and Broom were ready.

At nine o'clock Smith began to pace nervously.

At nine-forty-five Kelso went to the bathroom.

At nine-fifty-five Judge Boller put on his coat, hat, gloves, and scarf and inserted the earplug in his left ear. He put the leash on the poodle and went out the front door.

Kelso held his transmitter in sweaty hands and stood next to Smith, at the bay window of the dining room. The dining room lights were out. They saw Boller come around the side of the house with the dog, which strained impatiently at its leash, and continue as usual toward the rear. It was one minute before ten.

The telephone rang.

Smith grabbed up the extension. "Yes?" A pause, then he said to Kelso: "A man's in the alley."

Kelso swallowed hard.

"He's climbing over the fence," Smith said. "He's crawling into the evergreen tree."

Kelso peered out the window. The fresh snow glistened in the half-light. Judge Boller, the dog, and the tree cast long bluish black shadows over the whiteness. Kelso could see nothing in the tree, which looked thick and black.

"I can't see anything moving but the judge and the dog," he said.

"He's in the tree now," Smith said. Then, into the phone: "I'm hanging up now, Broom. Get ready." He replaced the receiver and came back to stand next to Kelso.

"Boller's at the tree," Kelso said, wiping first one hand and then the other on his corduroys.

"Why isn't anything happening?" Smith asked.

Then Kelso saw it. Almost unbelievably, a long thin object was emerging from the evergreen, just level with the judge's head. Boller stood sideways to the tree, almost exactly as his wife had stood, facing the alley. The stick came out of the tree and Kelso could make out some sort of dark object at the end of it. Within about ten seconds, the object was almost directly behind the judge's head.

"Come on, Kelso," Smith urged.

"Duck," Kelso said into the microphone.

Nothing happened.

"Duck!" Kelso said.

Judge Boller stood by the tree, ramrod stiff, shoulders back, head high, holding the leash in his left hand while the little black dog squatted in the snow. Kelso could see in sharp detail the dark tracks leading across the clean white snow, ending at the black boots of Boller and the tiny paws of the poodle.

"There must be something wrong with the earplug, or the transmitter," Kelso said. His heart pounded in his chest. He took a breath and yelled into the microphone: "Judge Boller! Duck! Get down!"

A bright reddish white flash appeared at the tip of the dark object on the stick. A fraction of a second later,

Kelso heard a sharp noise almost like a car backfiring, or a good-sized firecracker.

Boller pitched forward and sprawled facedown.

The black poodle ran. Its leash was still in the judge's left hand, and the dog was jerked off its feet. Then it got up, strained forward, and the leash came loose; it ran hard, making wide circles around the judge, who lay motionless in the snow.

"Jesus Christ," Smith muttered. And then, loudly: "Let's go!"

Kelso had frozen for an instant. Recovering, he hurried after Smith. They grabbed up their coats from kitchen chairs and put them on as they reached the back door. They ran out into the yard.

From across Agnes Street, a short dark figure and a tall round one trotted toward the tree.

The snow was deep and running was difficult. Kelso and Smith had their weapons out before they'd gotten five feet into the backyard. As they struggled toward the tree, it suddenly occurred to Kelso that they were sitting ducks against the white of the snow, but he kept going.

The stick was no longer visible. Another burst of light came from somewhere in the midsection of the evergreen branches, and this time the report came with it. He realized they were being shot at.

Meyer had reached the fence by now and was standing with his gun out. Broom was behind him and a few feet to the right.

"Come out of there!" Meyer shouted, his voice strangely high and shrill. Another shot, then Meyer crouched low on one knee and began firing into the tree.

"Don't kill him!" Kelso yelled.

"Are you nuts, Kelso?" Smith yelled, and started firing into the tree also.

Someone screamed, and the branches of the evergreen shook, as though some animal had run through them.

"Hold your fire," Kelso yelled. "Hold your fire!"

The shooting stopped. Kelso could hear sirens off in the

distance, over the ringing in his ears. They approached the tree cautiously. The little dog was whining, sniffing at its fallen master. They reached the tree—Meyer, Broom, Smith, and Kelso—and parted the lower branches, revolvers cocked and aimed.

A dark-haired man lay on the ground at the base of the tree, bleeding profusely from one arm and one shoulder. His eyes were wide and his features were distorted from pain or fear or both.

"Oh God," he said, in a high loud voice. "Don't kill me . . ."

"You're under arrest for murder," Meyer snapped.

Kelso backed away, turned, holstered his .38, and knelt in the snow next to the judge. Boller's head was turned to the left, exposing the ear into which the radio plug should have been inserted, but it wasn't there.

Boller's right arm was raised, so that his hand lay even with his head, and he seemed to be clutching something. Kelso spread the gloved fingers. An object lay there. It was the earplug.

The judge's eyes fluttered.

"Judge Boller?" Kelso bent low over him. "Your honor? Can you hear me?"

Smith came over and bent down on the other side.

Boller muttered something inaudible.

"He had the earplug in his hand," Kelso said. "No way for him to hear when I told him to duck."

Smith shook his head and looked disgusted.

"Why?" Kelso asked, speaking into the judge's ear.

Then he put his own ear near Boller's lips and listened. Through the ringing and the dog's barking and the approaching sirens, he heard Boller's low rasping voice.

"I did love her . . . Kelso . . ."

"Try to rest," Kelso told him, knowing it sounded absurd. "Help's coming."

The judge's lips moved. "Barbara . . ."

It was the last thing he said.

Forty-three

Donald Clark was the name of the man who had been shot from the tree. On the ground beside him was a curious object: a wooden pole, six feet long but with a locking metal hinge in the middle, so that it could be folded to only three feet for carrying. A .38 caliber revolver had been wired to one end, with a length of fishing line running from the trigger to a tack at the other end.

The wire holding the .38 had been loosened somewhat, in an apparent desperate effort to get the weapon off the stick.

Clark was taken to Clairmont General Hospital, and Kelso and Smith rode along with him in the ambulance. While a medic worked on the man's bullet wounds—one in the forearm, one in the shoulder, and one in the thigh—Clark grimaced and muttered things and suddenly peered up at Kelso, gritting his teeth.

"Try not to talk," the medic said.

"Is he . . . is he dead?" Clark asked.

Kelso nodded. "I'm afraid so."

Clark smiled; or it might have been a grimace.

"I'm glad," he said, speaking with an effort and breathing hard. "He . . . framed me. Said I raped Marilyn . . . I didn't . . . I let him use my apartment . . . cheating on his wife . . . sorry about his wife . . . thought it was him . . ."

"Just rest and stop talking," the medic said.

Clark closed his eyes. Then he opened them again and looked up at Kelso: "Did you find . . . key . . . I left on her coat?"

"Yes." Kelso nodded. "We found it. That's how we found you."

"Stupid." Clark lay back again, eyes closed. "Stupid . . . wanted to leave it . . . on Boller . . . leave the state . . . sorry about his wife . . ."

Then he was quiet.

"Will he be all right?" Kelso asked the medic.

"I don't think anything vital was hit."

Smith took out a cigarette, realized where he was, and put it away again. The siren was loud in the cramped quarters of the rear of the ambulance.

At Clairmont General, Clark was admitted to the emergency room and scheduled for immediate surgery. Kelso and Smith went to the coffee shop to wait, then thought better of it, assigned a uniformed officer to the job, and left.

A patrolman drove them back to the Municipal Building. They found Kelso's VW in the parking lot and headed toward Smith's apartment, not saying much.

"Boller took that earplug out on purpose," Kelso said finally.

"Yeah. I expect he did. The damned idiot."

"He must've realized he'd be killed."

"I never respect a man for taking the easy way out," Smith said.

"Apparently he felt responsible for his wife's death, after all. And letting Clark kill him, too, probably fit in with his idea of justice."

"Justice," Smith muttered.

At the apartment he got out and said: "See you tomorrow, Kelso."

"Good night."

Kelso drove home. The big yellow cat was waiting for him. He fed it and played with it for a few minutes, which made him feel a little better; then he phoned Susan.

"It's me. I'm home."

"George? What happened?"

"It's over." He told her about it.

"He shot at you? You could've been killed, George."

"Probably not. He couldn't get the gun loose from the end of the stick."

"What gave you the idea, anyway? About the stick?"

"Monkeys and bananas," he said.

And Susan, being Susan, chuckled and replied: "Of course!"

"I'm going to bed now," he told her. "I'll call you tomorrow."

"I love you, George."

"Yes," he said. "Me too." He hung up.

He drank a glass of milk and went upstairs. Showered and put on clean underwear. Climbed into bed. My own bed, he thought. My own pillow. He lay there for a while, his thoughts jumbled. Suddenly he thought of something, got up, went to his closet, and found the pair of pants he'd been wearing. He fished around in the pockets and found a blue metal key that did not belong to him. He'd forgotten to return it to Broom.

He put it on top of his chest of drawers and went back to bed. He slept well, and when he awoke the next morning, he felt refreshed.